SOMETHING
TO MAKE THE WORLD
A BETTER PLACE.

KITTY—A rich, beautiful American socialite . . . her Vassar education never taught her about evil . . . or the sacrifice required to destroy it.

STEVEN—A brave German officer . . . he thought he was serving his country and a dream, but he was only serving the twisted ambitions of the SS.

KRIEGSHOFER—The sadistic SS commander . . . his ambition was beyond limit, his racism beyond reason, his power beyond control.

RAMYAN LANGSUNG—A Tibetan monk . . . he held the key to the future in his mysterious knowledge of the past.

SOME WANTED TO DESTROY IT WITH . . .

THE PHOENIX FORMULA

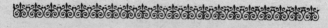

THE PHOENIX FORMULA

Tom Leighton

A DELL BOOK

Published by
Dell Publishing Co., Inc.
1 Dag Hammarskjold Plaza
New York, New York 10017

Dell ® TM 681510, Dell Publishing Co., Inc.

ISBN: 0-440-14649-6

Printed in the United States of America

First printing—November 1980

THE PHOENIX
FORMULA

Prologue

The haze drifting over the mountains of the Languedoc in the south of France as dusk settled over the
land was rank with spiraling black smoke. The stench
of burnt flesh, of blood, entrails and the hair of the
two hundred Cathar heretics massacred at the stake
drenched the slopes of Montségur, a burnt offering to
the now sacked and ruined citadel and temple. While
below, in the valley where the Pope's Crusaders from
the north had pitched their tents and unhitched the
trundle wagons of their whores, rose the cries of feasting, drinking and wenching and the roll of drums and
the shrill wails of their crude flutes.

The fall of the citadel of the Pures had come about
through treachery. A truce had been drawn up on the
first of March, 1244. The Cathars had read it, then
signed their names; the descendants of the barbarian
Clovis had scratched their marks. The thriving civilization of Toulouse with its poetry and art and trade
lay trampled by the north and its Catholic bishops.
On March 16 the citadel surrendered, the heretics
went to the stake, the conquerors feasted.

Yet a small band of Pures had succeeded in escaping
from the doomed citadel. Hidden in the grotto of

Bouan, they sat in torch-lit council as night brought them safety from pursuit.

The Elder finally rose and spoke. His face was drawn with fatigue, but his eyes glowed with his faith.

"Our hope lies now in heaven. Let us renounce our former lands and with it this world of matter and evil." The council murmured accord. The Elder had brought an end to their myriad plans to retake their kingdom, to restore their Church. In harmony with their faith they accepted this renunciation of the material world with relief. "Yet our Holy Grail must be kept out of the hands of the armies of Lucifer. One among us must forego his blessed death. The wisdom of our Grail must be kept from evil hands."

"Then choose among us, Father," declared the youngest, rising to his feet. As if in reply, all eyes were upon him. A young woman with red-blond hair next to him turned her face away. She had hoped to die with her knight, with this young priest whose sister she had become. Now she saw that this could not be. He was the chosen one.

The young man felt the eyes of the small band upon him. Quietly he looked from face to face. He would have liked to die with his brothers. He wanted to avoid his fate, but he knew that he could not.

"So be it," he uttered softly and sat down. The council kept silence, drifting into meditation almost as one mind.

The Elder broke their prayer. "We must plan now. Come, my son." Both the Elder and the young man rose and left the council. The young man followed the old one into the dark recesses of the grotto. In a crevice of rock lay a casket of silver small enough to be carried on the young man's back. In silence the young man knelt before the Elder as the old one strapped the casket securely to him, as he would a treasure to the back of a trusted stallion.

"I shall show you the way, my son." The young man

rose and followed. The casket felt light on his back. He picked up a staff, a cloak and a satchel of provisions as he went.

For nearly an hour they descended into the heart of the mountain. Suddenly the Elder stopped and turned back to the young man.

"Here I shall leave you. The path is true. God will protect you and His holy treasure." He bent forward and placed the kiss of peace on the young man's brow, then left him and followed the path back to the council under the flickering light of the torch.

"It has been done, my brothers." The Elder stood now before the council, which had not moved from the spot where he had left them. "We have all fasted. We are all pure for God. Let us forsake this world."

From the pocket of his vestment, he produced a silken pouch. He opened it and took out a pinch of the powdered herb which was contained inside; then, holding it in the palm of one hand, he passed the pouch along. From hand to hand it went. Each of the Pures, men and women, took their dosage from the pouch, until all had theirs in their hands and the pouch had returned to the Elder.

Without a moment's hesitation or doubt, they swallowed the powder in the palms of their hands. Then each one lay down on the floor of the grotto so that their bodies formed the spokes of a great wheel and, in a few minutes, lay dead.

Chapter One

As the taxi neared its destination, the sidewalks of the Yorkville section of Manhattan seemed to grow more congested. Pedestrians all appeared headed in a common direction. The address of the rally was correct, then. And people were coming to it.

The blue dusk of this early May evening was not very conducive to idle strolling. Spring had been unexpectedly cold that bleak year of 1933, as if to give a proper setting for the human weather of general unease: fear in some quarters, gloom sparked intermittently with the faint hopes of FDR's fireside soothsaying in all others.

These people, mostly of German extraction, were intent on something better. News from the fatherland, the old country, had recently become not only startling but euphoric, in sharp contrast to the news out of Washington. Letters from relatives were full of hope for the first time since the end of the Great War. On March 23 full powers had been given to Adolf Hitler, after his Nazi party had polled 43.9 percent of the vote in that month's elections. Few of them knew much about him; they were interested in knowing more.

In that Kitty Hammersmith was one with them. She peered out the taxi window at the men and women walking quickly, their hands thrust deep in their shabby coat pockets, their Germanic features tight with the seriousness of their goal: a meeting of the fledgling German-American Bund.

A small crowd spilled off into the street in front of the hired hall. The cabby was forced to slow down.

"This is fine." She pushed the door of the taxi open as it came to a halt, and stepped out. A gust of damp early evening air caught at her coat, snapping it against her legs, then billowing it open around her. As she turned back to pay the driver, she clutched the coat firmly to her.

Kitty was well into the throng as the cab inched away. A polite *bitte* here and there, a determined smile, got her what she wanted: a position as close to the speakers' dais as possible. Her Vassar-German-major skills had stood her in good stead.

She looked around the middle-size hall as she took a seat near the end of the third row. The only decoration was a large portrait of Adolf Hitler framed by two banners hung from the ceiling behind the speakers' platform. But there was considerable drama in this. The red banners emblazoned with the black swastika on a white circle were spotlit from below, creating a towering, magisterial effect.

Around her were ordinary-looking working people: a ramrod-straight older woman whom she had overheard praising Kitty's spirit, eagerness, strength and determination to her quiescent, portly husband as Kitty had made her way through the crowd; men and women with an apparent seriousness of purpose. They hardly seemed to be fanatics. In better times they would have been stalwart burghers, middle-class workers.

This made Kitty find them much more disturbing. By all reason these workers, these very people, should have rejected Hitler's vision and taken up the cause of the Left. Face to face with these people, it was more difficult to shrug them all off as *petits bourgeois*. They were the proletariat by all Marxist definition and, from their threadbare grimness, most seemed to be unemployed.

She had to be honest in her reporting. As the eyes and ears of a group of politically conscious young women at Vassar, who didn't live in New York as she did and weren't able to see this Bund meeting firsthand, she had to describe what she saw. Even if it didn't fit with their political theory.

The lights dimmed slightly, heightening the power of the swastika banners and the portrait of the new Führer. The crowd grew quieter.

At least she could report that it was a relatively small crowd, although the hall was filled to capacity.

And then Kitty felt a pair of eyes on her. She glanced diagonally toward the row behind her. A young man in an overcoat, hatless, revealing a tousled but military-looking haircut, smiled at her. His blue eyes were almost impertinent.

At that moment a man appeared behind the speaker's podium and the audience applauded politely, as one does at a concert where the mettle of the performers has not yet been tested but where much is expected. Kitty took the opportunity the speaker presented to turn her attention frontward, intent on ignoring the bold flirtation of those eyes behind her.

The speaker began in German, then stopped to ask in heavily accented English whether there were any objections. There were none. The man smiled broadly and continued. He was pleased to be among Germans here in America. Many Germans lived outside of the Fatherland, he continued. The German people had been betrayed, persecuted. But now all this would be righted. In a day soon to come, all Germans would be reunited in Germany.

There was mild, polite applause. Kitty thought she felt an air of uneasiness in many around her.

But the speaker continued. And then he introduced another speaker. The man expounded Nazi economic theory. The crowd grew slightly restive. The next speaker outlined recent German history, the triumphant march of the *Nationalsozialistische Deutsche Arbeiterpartei*, culminating in the events of March. The crowd showed interest but not enthusiasm.

Where, she wondered, was the impassioned demogoguery she had heard about? She could have been at a meeting of accountants.

And then the third speaker was introduced. He stood in silence for a full minute, appraising the audience. And then he began, his voice like a sudden clap of thunder: "German people, German race! Free yourself! Rise up against the swine, the Jews, who have ridden your backs up until this day! Come back with me to the early days of our Race, to the great forests and the massive mountain peaks of our ancestors, and feel the power of your—our—blood. It is from here that we shall march into the future and meet Victory! Let us go back now to those ancient days . . ."

The crowd sat riveted to the man's every word. Kitty found herself spellbound. So this was it. Later she would describe it as about equal to the magical, stentorian tones of the radio announcer calling up the legend of the Lone Ranger. But that would not really be accurate. The people around her, to a greater or lesser extent, were all moved by the voyage the speaker took them on through mythology, antiquity, mad racial theory, up to the glorious destiny of the Master Race.

The man received a standing, emotional ovation. He silenced them as the other speakers mounted the dais. Then he led them all in the new German national anthem. The small hall thundered with the fervor of their voices singing as one man: Germany over all else!

Kitty found her eyes welling with the emotion of it, chills running up and down her spine. She had never experienced the fervor of a crowd before. She would have to go to a union rally, she told herself.

And then it was over. People began filing out in couples and small groups. Their faces were flushed. Everyone seemed elated and talkative. The contrast with the dour tenor of the crowd only an hour before was devastating.

As Kitty edged out of her row, she felt a hand on her coat sleeve.

"Hello. Wasn't it marvelous?" The young man spoke to her in English. Kitty looked around to catch people's reactions. Apprehensive, she felt that she was being singled out as a spy of sorts. But no one paid any attention. Of course young German-Americans would speak to each other in English.

"Yes, it was." She smiled at him. Somehow the high spirits in the hall made his forwardness natural. She was surprised at her own reaction; her reply had the ring of truth. But then there *was* something marvelous about what she had just witnessed.

"You aren't with someone, are you?" His blue eyes clouded slightly.

She hesitated. "No, I'm not, but I've got to get right home. My mother's waiting up for me . . ." It was a lie. Her mother was at a dinner party. Kitty had only gotten out of the formal affair by claiming a headache. Gertrude Winslow Hammersmith would have given her hell if she had had any idea of what Kitty had been up to. Her politics were Republican if anything at all. She did not much approve of women in politics or of their being interested in them very much. She only vaguely knew the difference between Left and Right. Actually she found it all a bore and, in the end, not very important for their sort. Kitty's natural father might have disagreed, but he was dead; her stepfather agreed in principle, but doted on Kitty much too much to push the matter any further. He found anything his Vassar stepdaughter did charming and a source of pride, but business matters took up a great deal of his time now, and Kitty saw him rarely. At that very moment he was in Chicago somewhere, trying to put together some capitalist scheme. And he would probably meet with success. While others foundered, he kept them all safe from the Depression in their Fifth Avenue apartment overlooking Central Park.

"Oh . . . I was hoping you'd have a cup of coffee with me." He looked at her sadly, respectfully.

His expression put the devil in her. She glanced at her watch. "I think a drink would be much more fun." She slipped her hand around his arm.

His look of shocked surprise was worth it all. As they emerged onto the sidewalk and into the chill night air, she noted a feeling of hesitation coming from him. And then he blurted it out.

"You won't believe this, but, you know, I don't really know any speakeasies. I'm from out of town." He was lying. He and his West Point chums knew plenty of speakeasies in New York, but not any of the smart ones, ones suitable for a young lady.

"I thought you were from around here. From York-ville. You look German." Her surprise was genuine.

"Yes, I am German. But I'm not from Yorkville."

"Oh, well, that doesn't matter." Full of her impulse, she flagged down a taxi. "Get in. I know some swell ones." She opened the door for him, but that was too much; he insisted she go first. Inside, she leaned forward and gave the address to the driver, then sat back, pleased with herself. He got in and shut the door after him, and they were off toward Park Avenue.

"You seem to be a girl who knows her way around."

She nodded. "I guess I am. Does that bother you?" She kept her eyes directed steadfastly at the people and buildings rapidly being left behind. What had possessed her to take this stranger off to a speakeasy?

"Not at all." But he could see that she was having second thoughts. "I like a woman who knows what she wants."

"Oh, do you now." She turned to face him. "If you think what I want includes going to bed with you, you're in for a shock."

"Wait a minute, Miss . . ." He paused to let her fill in her name, but she said nothing. "What right do you—How do you know why I asked you out for a—"

"I wasn't born yesterday."

"Never thought you were."

"Well, if you must know, I found you good-looking and I thought it would be interesting." She looked abruptly back out the window to hide a look of despair. What mess had she gotten into now?

A smile crept over his face. "I couldn't keep my eyes off you." His voice was soft and romantic.

She turned and looked at him. Then she burst into laughter.

His face reddened instantly. "I don't think there's anything funny in that!"

"No. No, there's nothing funny." She couldn't control her laughter. "It's just that . . ." She took hold of herself. "No, no. I'm sorry. I'm just laughing at us. At the whole situation."

He immediately relaxed and smiled. "I guess it is kind of silly."

"Yes, it is. Look, we're here!" The taxi slowed. "Anywhere here, driver." The cab stopped and Kitty stepped out. The young man followed, reached into his pocket and paid the driver. As the taxi sped off, he looked around. It was a fashionable block off Park Avenue.

"I'd never have thought there'd be a speakeasy in a neighborhood like this."

"The rich like to drink, too, silly. Come on." She led him a few steps up the block, then down to a basement-level door below a respectable-looking brownstone. She knocked, and the typical trap window opened. Then the door opened and they went in.

A small jazz band played soft and low. The place was a collection of café tables with a small dance floor and lots of tinsel and white plaster. It was half-empty. They gave the coat-check girl their things, and the maitre d' led them to a table. He seated Kitty while the young man sat down opposite her, then stood expectantly.

The young man felt uneasy. "It's not very crowded tonight."

"It's early yet. Let's have champagne."

"Do they have the real thing here?"

The maitre d' cleared his throat.

"Of course they do."

"I assure you, monsieur, it is only the very best."

"In that case then, *garçon*, a bottle of champagne."

"I'll send the waiter immediately, monsieur."

Kitty laughed as the maitre d' marched off briskly. "I don't think he appreciated being called *garçon*."

"He's a pompous fool. Here it's just a speakeasy, not Paris and the Ritz Bar."

Kitty nodded to placate him. "I didn't mean to criticize. You're right, he is a pompous ass. Do you know the Ritz Bar in Paris?"

"Yes, I do. My father always stays at the Ritz when he's in Paris; I've met him there."

"You *are* from out of town." A touch of sarcasm lay under the emphasis.

"I'm German. My father's German. We live in Berlin." Kitty was startled; she had figured him to be of German descent, but American.

"You don't seem to have any accent."

"My mother's American. But she died years ago. I was born here, but we went back to Germany—my father and I, that is. My secondary education was in Berlin. But I had a chance to get into West Point and my father thought it a good idea . . ." He hesitated; he had not meant to tell her about West Point. "You must speak German, too. Are you . . . ?"

"One hundred percent American, whatever that means. I've studied German."

"In college?"

"Yes, at Vassar. How did you know?"

"You act like a college girl."

"And how does a college girl act?"

"Like the world's her oyster. And, in your case, Miss . . ."

"Kitty."

"In your case, Kitty, it certainly is. My name's Stefan. Like Steven over here."

The waiter arrived with the champagne, set down two glasses and uncorked the bottle. As the froth subsided in her glass, Kitty raised it. "What shall we toast to?"

Stefan hesitated. He wasn't much good at proposing toasts. "To us."

"To our hopes and aspirations." Kitty then clinked her glass against his and took a long sip. "Oh, I love champagne."

"Spoken like a true debutante."

"What an interesting discovery on your part." Her voice was again tinged with sarcasm. She despised the whole notion of "the debutante," as well as the class of people who had invented it.

"You're very touchy, aren't you. I didn't mean anything by it. I would have thought you'd—"

"Wrong again. I've learned that people just aren't always what they seem, haven't you?" Her tone was blatantly patronizing, but he ignored that. It had struck a responsive cord in him, as if it were the truth behind why they were now sitting face to face, talking in this absurdly belligerent way. And then the flash of insight vanished before he could get a hold on it. He was left with an oddly puzzled expression on his face.

Kitty laughed. "Well, don't take it all that seriously. Let's dance." She stood up.

He rose slowly after her. "I just thought of something, and then it disappeared before . . . I thought for a moment I understood why we'd met."

She slipped her hand around his arm. She was about to laugh off his remark as overly serious, then caught herself. "I know."

But as they danced, she realized that she didn't know at all. There was something uncanny about their meeting, but what it was escaped her. She turned the conversation to something she thought would be useful to talk about. "What did you think of the meeting?"

"The first part . . ." he began.

"Was deadly boring."

He laughed at her interruption. "Yes, but the last speaker . . ." He had turned very serious.

"I imagined him to be a lot like Herr Hitler. That way with a crowd."

"No. It's much more than that, don't you see? He was talking about destiny. About the future of Germany and all Germans."

"You don't swallow all that racial nonsense, do you?"

He almost stopped dancing. "Why, if you think it's nonsense, why, I guess I do. I believe in Germany. There's something powerful and right . . . It confirmed my decision."

"And what was that?" She was put off guard by his ardor; she hadn't expected this. In a way he disappointed her, as did anyone she liked who did not share her liberal views. But by the same token, he became fascinating.

"To return at once to Germany. To a country that needs a good military man, that respects one. I want to be part of that future Germany." His voice was impassioned.

The song ended. In silent agreement they returned to their table. It would be easier to talk there.

"Aren't you taking a terrible risk? I thought West Point graduates were required to do military service."

Stefan emptied his glass and poured another, refreshing hers. He drank half of the new one down. There was grim determination on his face.

"I don't know why I'm discussing this with you, but—there's no real army here, no respect for one, no money for one. In Germany that will be different. Germany is on the rise. America?" He laughed bitterly. "In a year it'll be in the hands of the Jews and the Reds."

"That's quite a statement!" She began to laugh but thought better of it. She did not want to anger him; she was somehow afraid to. "And you'll give up your American citizenship," she stated, rather than asked, softly.

"Without a second thought." He emptied his glass.

They sat in silence. She watched him as he stared at the linen tablecloth and carved lines in it with his fingernail. Then suddenly he looked up at her. "I thought you'd understand. You were there tonight. Didn't you feel anything?"

She had to turn her gaze away from the intense questioning of his eyes. She hesitated. She did not want to go into her own theories—dare she even call them beliefs?—about the world. They had none of the certainty of his.

"It's different. I'm not German."

"Oh, no, don't you see? That's not the point. You're Aryan. You aren't a Jew. I can tell that—"

"Can you?" Her laughter followed, but it had no gaiety to it. "I think I'd better get home. I told my mother I had a headache so I could get out of going to a dinner party with her. She doesn't approve much of women interested in politics. In fact, she doesn't think much of politics, period." She stood up.

Stefan looked up at her before slowly rising to his feet. "I've said something wrong. Can't we finish the bottle together?"

"I must get home." She smiled at him and shook her head. "I'll get hell if I don't."

"And you just walked out!" Helen laughed. "You haven't changed a bit."

Kitty put the last pin in her hair and gave her coiffure a satisfied appraisal in the mirror.

"Oh, I haven't, have I? Well, for your information, I'm six years older and wiser."

"Ain't we all, honey." The two women laughed together. Helen got up from her perch on the edge of Kitty's bed, took a cigarette out of her bag and lit it. She strutted slowly across the room, swaying to the rhythm of the swing tune on the radio. She took a puff of her cigarette. "And you think it's the same guy?"

"Your guess is as good as mine. I never got his last name. But he is Wehrmacht and was West Point. How many of those creatures can there be walking around these days?"

Helen shook her head. She was short and dark with a good figure, but she knew she didn't have Kitty's appeal, her cool, tall beauty that demanded high fashion to enhance it even further. "It could only happen to a gal like you."

"Oh, come off it, Helen. Let's not go into that lucky-rich-girl story again."

"Well, at least you're not a Jew like me. *Oy veh's mir!*" Helen burst into a howl of laughter.

Kitty laughed and shook her head.

"You don't think I should make a joke like that, do you, Kitty?" Helen had become immediately serious.

"I don't see how you can, that's all. Considering everything that's happening." She walked over to Helen's purse on the bed. "Can I bum a cigarette?" Kitty reached in and pulled one out and lit it. She didn't really like to smoke but when she was nervous, it calmed her.

Helen shrugged. "It's the best I can do. You're lucky. You can go off and do something. Me? If I don't look Jewish, who does?"

The voice of Father Charles Edward Coughlin had replaced the swing music on Kitty's bedroom radio. They hadn't noticed until then. Helen rolled her eyes heavenward. "That's him, isn't it? Can I turn that thing off?" Her voice was flat and sarcastic. She moved toward the radio.

"You mean to tell me, Helen, you've never heard him?"

"Don't torture me." Helen's hand reached for the dial.

"No, wait. You should at least hear what he's like."

"Yeah, and I should sleep on a bed of nails and play 'Deutschland Über Alles' for a lullaby." But Helen took her hand off the dial. She began to listen with the fascination of a victim for the executioner. The priest was talking about the situation in Europe, about the danger of the Reds, and then came back to turf more familiar to his audience: America, 1938. The dangers were just as real here in the good old USA. International Jewry in the form of Jewish bankers and arms merchants wanted to drive the world to war . . .

"That's about all I can take." Helen turned the dial.

Kitty laughed. "All right. But at least you've heard."

"Fascinating." Benny Goodman's clarinet filled the room. Helen looked around for an ashtray and, not finding one, threw her half-smoked cigarette into the fireplace. "You know, if you're so keen on being objec-

tive, I can't see why you're sticking your neck out. If
they ever find you out, honey . . ."

Kitty laughed. "Don't be silly. As you said, I'm the
perfect Aryan specimen."

"That won't matter if they suspect that it's you
who—"

"They won't, Helen. They just won't. Now let's end
it there." There was anger in her voice. She had made
her decision; she had volunteered. "Anyway—" her
voice was calmer now; she sat down on the bed. "What
have I got to lose?"

Helen rolled her eyes. "Nothing but a couple of mil-
lion and a ten-room apartment overlooking the Park."

"That's not mine. It was Mother's. It was my father's. I did nothing for it. It means nothing to me."

"You're out of your head."

She paced the room, clutching the phone to her ear.
The tub was slowly filling with hot water. The bath-
oil bubbles foamed into great billows as the steam rose
into the white and black tiled bathroom. But she only
heard the voice over the telephone.

"I can't believe she'd do anything that stupid . . .
Which hospital? . . . I'll get a cab . . . No. No, I
haven't changed my mind. If anything . . . All right.
Thank you. Thank you for calling." She hung up. She
stood stunned in the middle of the bedroom, indiffer-
ent to the rapidly filling tub. It made no sense. What
had possessed Helen to go to one of the Bund meetings?

They were a far cry from the first one she had attended out of vague curiosity six years before. They
were now mammoth, policed by goon squads trained
in various camps in New York and New Jersey. And
the crowds they attracted were enormous, almost as
large as the ones back in the *Vaterland*.

Suddenly Kitty remembered the tub. She dashed

into the bathroom. Already the bubbles were spilling onto the floor, but the water was only at the brim.

The phone rang again.

Her whole body stiffened in fear. She already knew the message of the call. Slowly she went back into her bedroom and picked up the receiver after the fourth ring. "Hello. Yes . . . Oh my God, yes. Yes. Somehow I . . . Yes, I'll call back later." She hung up. Helen was dead. Concussion. Coma. Death.

Kitty sat down on the edge of the bed. Death was no stranger, as it was to most other people. Funny. Terror suddenly froze her body. A choked cry escaped from her throat. And then it was over. Tears welled up and rolled down her cheeks. She began to sob. She had loved Helen. When the small Piper Cub had crashed in Montana, ending her parents' holiday on the vast W.B. Ranch, Helen had been there for her. Three years had passed and now Helen, too, was gone.

She allowed herself to weep freely until the tears wouldn't come anymore, and then she got up and went into the bathroom. She took a tissue from the vanity and dried her eyes and blew her nose. She slipped off her robe, hung it up on the hook on the back of the door and sunk into the steaming tub.

What had before been a fine mixture of reason and ideals and sense of purpose, had now passed into the realm of vengeance, of fanaticism and of destiny. Now she would go to Berlin for the sake of her own soul. There was no choice but Berlin.

In the steaming tub a cold shudder shook through her body which she knew immediately as the first inkling of her own mortality.

Chapter Two

"I don't think you love me anymore, Stefan." Helga pushed him an inch away from her to emphasize her oft-repeated accusation. She was tall, blond, of impeccable Aryan stock—as anyone with two eyes could tell—perfect for the role of wife of a fast-rising officer in the Wehrmacht. She made him miss a step of the fox-trot.

"Perhaps you're right. I think we should sit down," he replied wearily. Stefan Blauer had no intention of marrying this perfect specimen of Aryan womanhood, only of making love to her. And of late he was not sure he even wanted to do that. He moved as if to stop dancing, but Helga snuggled up closer to him and continued to follow his now imaginary steps. To save embarrassment Blauer started up again.

"You're heartless—nothing but an animal," she hissed in his ear, while her face appeared blissfully romantic. The charade she played to the world that they were a couple ideally in love was of vital importance to her. Having an officer-lover meant a nice flat in a fashionable Berlin neighborhood, the latest Paris fashions and dinner invitations to the homes of the powerful. She knew that Blauer had grown tired of her. In order not to lose her position, however, it would have to seem that she had thrown him over in favor of another officer. She had one picked out already, seated at a table not far from that of Stefan's party. His eyes had watched her hungrily all evening. And now she gave him a wink from across the dance floor. The man replied with a stiff Prussian nod and a flashing smile full of impeccable white teeth. This unknown officer was much more her match, she noted with delight, much more of a real man—heavier, with a promising bull-like neck—than the long-limbed, aristocratic-looking Stefan. Anyway, she took no interest in manners and brains, only in power.

"We had better sit down." Stefan stopped abruptly. He pulled away from her and gave her his arm to escort her back to their table. The bull-necked officer watched the couple leave the dance floor with keen interest. Obersturmführer Vebel wanted the woman Helga, but only so long as she continued to be Blauer's mistress.

An older civilian gentleman and three other Wehrmacht officers stood up as Stefan seated Helga at the table.

"A nice turn on the floor, you two." Hans von Eschenberg smiled at them, acting as elder statesman or jovial old uncle as the changing situation of the evening required. The starched crispness of his wing-tipped collar served to further emphasize his tall, gray-haired elegance. His evening clothes contrasted sharply with the dress uniform of the officers. He epitomized the values of the aristocracy, or so it seemed in a club mostly frequented by newly powerful if somewhat boorish Party officials. Even the fox-trot bore a trace of beer-hall oom-pah-pah sentimentality. It was what was now popular in Berlin's chicest night spots; Weimar decadence with its jazzier notes had been supplanted by sturdier, more Germanic chords.

Von Eschenberg's position in the Reich was basically ceremonial, as was his role at the table. He was a Hindenburg: a symbol that within the new Nazi order lay continuity and German civilization.

Once he had believed that it did. Recently, however, he had come across disturbing facts—even in his position in the Ministry of Culture—which sharply contradicted this. As an aristocrat of dying lineage, he had not felt the least bit compromised by the death of the Republic, but the death of certain values—Western, Christian values—disturbed him. The compromising of these had compromised everything.

Watching Helga cross the room with Stefan had brought all this home. Now with well-bred, old-fashioned sophistication, Hans set such thoughts aside and continued smiling at the young couple as they sat down. Helga was bright-eyed, a beautiful blond creature—as usual. But he caught a look of pique, quickly camouflaged, in Stefan that told him that his young protégé, born of an American woman he had never met and of a great and good old friend, now dead, was ready to throw over this mistress. Von Eschenberg would not mourn Helga's passing. He had never cared for any of Stefan's women.

The fox-trot was over. The lights in the nightclub dimmed so that the deco curves and columns and shallow flights of stairs from one level to another took on an eerie glow. A spotlight suddenly pinpointed center stage.

"*Mesdames et messieurs . . .*" The master of ceremonies, a short man in evening clothes with a pencil-line mustache that gave him the desired French air, announced the main show—a very popular songstress with a deep, throaty voice. The room broke into applause, bringing the tall, leggy blond singer in a shimmering sheath gown onto the stage. She bowed mannishly as the orchestra started up the introduction to her first number. Through the languid strings, her deep voice began: "*Der Wind hat mir ein Lied erzählt*

. . . " The audience gasped and applauded with pleasure.

Von Eschenberg caught a passing waiter and ordered champagne. Within minutes all at the table silently toasted. Helga snuggled up against Stefan as she glanced over to the table where her new interest sat. She was delighted to find the SS first lieutenant staring at her. He now averted his eyes and looked away as if ashamed of his boldness. Stefan drew back from Helga. Instantly a puzzled expression appeared, then vanished from Vebel's face.

"Don't be like that, darling," she whispered fiercely in Stefan's ear.

"Excuse me, I need a pack of cigarettes." Before anyone could reply, Stefan was on his feet and slipping back into the lounge.

Stefan Blauer could feel the surprised looks of his table companions on him, following him as he moved among the other tables to the back of the club. He was not himself. Moodiness, changeability were not his style. And he was not the kind of man to get upset by a woman. He did not make scenes and did not care to witness them.

Now, as he took a seat in the rear of the lounge and lit a cigarette from an almost full pack, his hand trembled. He looked at it with a mixture of amazement and disgust. So the SS could break his nerve.

Von Eschenberg watched Stefan move away from the table with a look of undisguised worry.

"It's the meeting tomorrow," muttered Krug, a ruddy-faced young officer with slicked-back reddish-blond hair.

Von Eschenberg turned to him and nodded. The singer finished her song, followed by near-deafening applause. Von Eschenberg had to speak up. "How much do you know about this, Herr Krug?"

"Totally unexpected." He shrugged his shoulders with a wry grin. "But isn't that their way, the black-shirted bastards. First-rate theatrics, but could they fight a battle like a military man? The Führer keeps them for the dirty work at home, for dealing with Reds and Jews. But it's army men that the Führer is going to need in the end."

Von Eschenberg nodded. "Quite so. Quite so, my good friend." But his mind was elsewhere. Krug was no fool. He was clever enough to figure out a political move if there were any clues at all. Obviously, then, there were none. Which made von Eschenberg even more certain that the summons Stefan Blauer had received from the SS High Command to go to the mountain retreat not far from Berchtesgaden the very next afternoon had a great deal to do with Gerd Blauer. If not everything.

Von Eschenberg only liked to remember Gerd, Stefan's father, from the old days, before '32. From 1932 until his car accident in '33, his great old friend had become a stranger. Gerd had been dead six years already, then, sighed von Eschenberg. But for him he had been dead seven. May he rest in peace. If in the universe peace could be found.

"I think I should go look for Stefan." Helga's announcement came so suddenly that the men at the table jerked to their feet, only to watch her vanish among the other tables.

The orchestra struck up a faster, more militaristic tempo. The audience applauded as they recognized the song, and the singer began. Before her deep, tremulous voice had sung of love calling on the winds. Now she sang of the battle of love, of life for love. Von Eschenberg felt himself become the detached observer. Stefan's friends at the table glowed with rapture; the entire room was stirred by the call to sacrifice. He had seen these expressions before, in 1914. There was no mystery. It was a quick step from love today to war tomorrow. Nineteen thirty-nine would be a year for the world to reckon with.

Helga scanned the table where the *Obersturmführer* had sat as she went ostensibly in search of Stefan, but her admirer had gone. The appreciative looks she received from other uniformed men only partially placated her; she was more captivated by her unknown admirer than she had thought.

She entered the lounge, certain of finding Stefan quietly smoking. He was not there. She stopped in the middle of the floor, not sure of what to do next. She felt suddenly that all eyes were on her, that everyone knew she had been jilted. She composed a look of purpose on her face and headed for a sofa. She sat down as if she had only briefly forgotten that all she wanted in the world at that moment was to sit down in the lounge.

So it was all over with Stefan. Fine, she was bored with him. He was too young, too idealistic for her taste. But she did not like the fact that he had been the one to call an end to their affair. Because it was finished. She knew which gestures were only a spat; which marked the true end. The words were sure to follow, if not that evening, then the next day. Still she had been caught off guard.

"May I sit down, *Fräulein?*" The assured male voice startled her out of her cold appraisal of her situation.

"How could a woman refuse an answered prayer?" She had the extraordinary, catlike gift of always landing on her feet, she noted to herself with sharp pride.

"And how is this, *gnädiges Fräulein?*" smiled the bull-necked officer. Her words, her manner, came as a surprise.

"Simply that I summoned you up, and there you are. But I don't think we have been introduced, lieutenant." She remarked his SS rank. Her boldness turned into a demure pout.

"May I take it upon myself?"

"By all means . . ." Her laughter was light, coquettish.

Blauer had not wanted to go back to his table after finishing his cigarette. He felt too out of control. Helga was sure to do or say something that would make him lose his temper. He insisted on a cool, quiet termination of the affair. Frankly, he now felt her not worth the energy that would be expended in anger. After the raging lust he had had for her body, after her sensual, animal ways in bed, he now felt nothing for Helga. She had ceased to exist as a real person for him. She was just another pretty doll; there were plenty more who liked the look of a man in uniform. And after all, he realized with amusement, wouldn't Helga look much more stunning on the arm of a black-uniformed SS man?

The irony of the question on this, the eve of his summons by the SS, did not escape him. Blauer headed for the bar. A whiskey and water was what he needed.

Officers—SS, Wehrmacht, Luftwaffe—caroused in groups or leaned on the bar next to studiedly glamorous, expensive women in long evening gowns. In his present mood Blauer would have ordered his drink without a second look at any of them. But one of them stood out. She looked familiar—a young woman with wavy auburn hair pinned up in the back for the evening and wearing a fuller, more youthful-looking gown that made him think she was a foreigner, an American. She was staring at him. Having caught his eye, she seemed to blush. She turned away to take a sip of her drink. Then her eyes returned to meet his with a candid interest that was in marked contrast to the usual wanton seductiveness of the other women in the place. Blauer was charmed. Her eyes riveted him so that he found the bartender staring at him impatiently, waiting for his order.

"Whiskey and water, *bitte*." He started to ask the bartender who the girl was, then thought better of it. She was different from the others there; he would ask her himself.

The singer ended her show as Stefan took a first sip of his drink. The applause was thunderous. But there was no encore, and the lights went up. Dance music began: a fast waltz. In a rush of nostalgia, couples filled the dance floor. Blauer looked down the bar toward the girl. An SS officer had turned and was speaking to her. Blauer sensed that she was not enjoying his attentions; it was his chance.

"Excuse me, *mein Hauptsturmführer*, the young lady promised me this dance." Blauer turned to the girl with a conspiratorial smile. "Did you not?" She seemed to hesitate. Perhaps she didn't know German.

"Another time, *mein Herr*?" She turned and spoke to the SS man in a nearly flawless German accent. The *Hauptsturmführer* bowed curtly, barely hiding his contempt and anger at Blauer. They were of equal rank—captain—if not of the same service.

"Perhaps, *Fräulein*. Perhaps." He abruptly turned back to his cronies.

"Rude man, isn't he?" said Kitty Hammersmith as Stefan escorted her to the dance floor.

Stefan laughed. "That's a very succinct way of putting it, *Fräulein*." Blauer introduced himself.

"Kitty Hammersmith from New York . . . I'm American," she added as if to clarify any confusion.

"Then I was right."

"Were you? Is it that obvious?" They began dancing. He laughed and shook his head.

"Don't you remember me?"

"Should I?" Her dark blue eyes twinkled.

Blauer was entranced. She must remember. She was too relaxed with him. She was toying.

"Well, I think so. What was the year—1933? New

York. A cold spring evening. The German-American Bund. A speakeasy."

"Sounds terribly romantic, doesn't it?"

"It was." He laughed. "I've never forgotten you."

"Oh?" She obviously didn't believe him. "Maybe you've got the wrong girl."

He felt a momentary doubt. "I don't think there could be that many German-speaking girls named Kitty in New York."

She laughed. "Of course I remember you."

And there he was face to face with a girl he had barely known for a half-hour six years ago. Yet he felt she knew more about him than any of his mistresses. "So, here we are. You haven't changed. Oh, but maybe. You're more beautiful."

She smiled. "And you've got even more of a line." But she edged a bit closer to him as they danced, closing her eyes and resting her cheek on his shoulder. He tightened his arms around her. It seemed impossible, yet they were dancing as if six years were just the other day. What were the odds for this kind of thing? And she was even more beautiful.

They danced in silence, letting the music and their movements speak for them. The waltz ended with quiet applause from the dancers. Then the band struck up a South American tempo.

"Let's sit this one out, shall we?" There was no trace of an order in his voice, but he remembered suddenly how she had liked taking the lead.

"You don't like the samba?" She laughed lightly as she put her arm in his.

He was relieved. He wanted to please her. To his surprise there was a desperateness he had never felt before about his desire to please.

They returned to the bar. The tables had to be avoided. He didn't want a confrontation with Helga now, not at this delicate point. After all these years.

But he hoped Helga would see them, it would make the break easier.

"Frankly, I haven't the slightest interest in South America."

"That's funny." She picked up her drink. "I read somewhere that lots of Germans, especially top Nazis, had a great deal invested in South America."

She didn't have to wait long for a reaction. It was instantaneous.

"Pure propaganda by Jews and Reds, Kitty." He frowned and took up his drink. He changed the subject. "Do you still go to Bund meetings?"

"Yes." She could reply truthfully.

"And do you really believe your leader, Bundführer Kuhn, is guilty of stealing Bund funds, as your Bolshevik-ridden government has charged?" A smile of satisfaction played on his face. He had her there. She looked away. She had to think fast.

"Yes." Her voice was weary. Her eyes were sad. "Yes. I'm afraid I do."

Hans von Eschenberg had caught sight of Stefan Blauer leading a young woman to the dance floor long before the others at the table did. It was unfortunate, he thought, that Helga was not at the table with them. He would have liked to have seen her reaction. He realized suddenly that he detested her and was surprised at the intensity of his contempt.

"Isn't that Blauer?" nudged Horst Gruber, *Oberleutnant*, the other officer at the table along with Krug. Von Eschenberg nodded with one eyebrow arched in amusement. In a minute Krug also had spotted Blauer. Before the red-faced Lieutenant Krug could blurt out his discovery they both nodded to him, then burst out laughing. Krug was always the last to see, the last to know. Not sure of whether they were laughing at him or at his discovery, Krug blushed a shade redder, but joined in the laughter.

"So, one down and a new one in her place," put in Krug as soon as he could be heard.

"It would seem so, would it not?" Von Eschenberg followed his words with a fatherly smile at Krug, followed in turn by a sigh to keep up paternal appearances.

Krug nodded, pleased with himself.

"And it would seem that she has solved Blauer's jitter problem," added Horst.

"So it would seem." She was pretty, Von Eschenberg noted to himself. And he guessed that she was foreign, though he could not tell what nationality. He doubted, however, whether Stefan had truly forgotten about his command performance for the SS.

Would they bring up the subject of Gerd Blauer? That would give young Blauer quite a jolt, especially if they went into detail.

No, he realized, they would not compromise themselves or the mission. Perhaps he should warn Stefan. But what could he say? There would be plenty of time afterward. He did not want to play his own hand so early in the game.

No, talk of Gerd Blauer would only lead to embarrassing implications for the Totenkopf faction of the SS. They could not bring it up. He chuckled to himself. They would be in quite a pickle trying to explain to Stefan why he had been chosen for such a bizarre assignment—that is, if Hans was correct in his assumption of what it was. Someone as rational as Stefan, with his no-nonsense military kind of mind, would find it all ridiculous. Von Eschenberg shook his head to himself, but no one at the table noticed.

"How would you like to go somewhere else, Kitty?"
"Why not get a table?"

Stefan tried to hide his annoyance. "That wouldn't be very practical."

Kitty laughed. "I bet it wouldn't. Who was the young lady? The blond wrapped around you on the dance floor?"

"You mean, damn it, that you saw me, knew it was me all that time?" His military training told him that offense was the best defense.

Kitty laughed again. "Oh, I wasn't sure at first. Who is she, Stefan?"

"My former mistress." He took a defiant sip of his drink and faced Kitty. She met his challenge with an eye-to-eye gaze. Then they both laughed.

"Do you run through women that fast?"

"I do when they're that kind."

She turned away slightly. "Oh, I see." Then she turned back to him. "How's your father, Stefan?" He was surprised. Stefan smiled and put his glass down on the bar.

"I never saw him. He died the day before we docked in Hamburg. Auto accident."

"Oh, I'm sorry, Stefan." She reached out and touched his arm. Her sympathy was all too genuine. She smiled gently, then, ironically, raised her glass. "Here's to two orphans." She took a sip. "Finally we have something real to toast. Remember that last one—the one you had a hard time coming up with?"

He touched her glass with his, then drained it. "Yes, I do. I'm not much better at it now."

Silence followed. For a moment Kitty looked away, her eyes taking in the shadowed contours, the steps, the palms, the men and women in evening dress, the officers in uniform, the cold glamour of the club. During that time Stefan devoured her with his eyes. Kitty was more than beautiful, stylish, clever—she was startlingly lovable to him. Something in her struck a chord of truth, of honesty between them—as if they could not lie to each other.

"What are you staring at, Stefan? Did I spill some-thing on my dress?" But she didn't look at her dress. Her eyes twinkled with humor and caught him up in it.

"Let's go out for supper somewhere." He almost whispered it. He realized suddenly that he was terri-fied she might say no.

"Do you actually know of a place this time?" She laughed. "You didn't last time, remember."

"Plenty of places, Kitty. Marvelous ones." He gave her his arm.

Obersturmführer Vebel stiffened noticeably as he caught sight of Stefan Blauer crossing the lounge with a girl—a foreigner, so it would seem—on his arm.

Helga's eyes immediately followed his. She was not surprised at what she saw. Grudgingly she admired Stefan for his forcefulness, his directness. It was per-fect. She could have written the script herself.

"Stefan!" she called out to him and stood up. "Please take me home."

Blauer stopped dead in his tracks. He had almost forgotten Helga's existence. His normally cool, calm face tensed now and reddened, but his first embarrass-ment turned swiftly to anger. The bratty, demanding expression on Helga's face, her obvious pleasure at em-barrassing him by making a scene in public, came to-gether before his eyes like a concrete thing, a set of old shackles which he would now shatter once and for all.

"I believe you have your own escort, my dear Helga. Good night." Stefan directed his eyes perfunctorily at the SS officer. "Lieutenant, *heil Hitler!*" He saluted. Vebel stood at attention and saluted his Wehrmacht superior: *"Mein Hauptmann, heil Hitler!"*

"Come on, Kitty." Stefan nudged her gently as she stood stunned by the unexpected scene. She smiled up at him immediately and nodded. She had been watch-

ing the encounter with a mixture of amazement and
humor. Now she averted her eyes from Helga and her
SS officer as they left the club.

Helga sat down as if pulling herself abruptly back
into her seat.

"Well, I hope," she began with an acid tone still in
her voice as she turned to the officer, "all you men are
not so fickle and . . . and ill-mannered."

The bull-necked officer smiled slowly to himself,
then rose smoothly to his feet. He stood before Helga
in a half-bowing pose.

"'All you men?' Precisely, *mein fräulein*; there are
perhaps too great a number of men in your life. So
confusing, no? Good night, Fräulein Helga. We shall
meet soon again, I hope. A pleasure." With a short
bow conceived partly to conceal the amused look on
his face, he turned on his heels and left her. He could
now chuckle to himself as he crossed the lounge. She
was of absolutely no interest to him now.

Instead of going to his table, he stopped at the bar.
The bartender approached.

"The foreign girl, what is her nationality?" Vebel
inquired.

"American."

"You know this for sure?" Vebel smiled.

"Her name is Kitty Hammersmith from New York.
And a rich one at that." The bartender flashed a conspiratorial smile.

"Interesting, then," smiled back Obersturmführer
Vebel. He turned and left the bar. It was almost too
easy, he thought to himself.

Chapter Three

The great banquet hall before him was blinding in its whiteness. Lighted by hundreds of white candles planted in great iron rings suspended from the ceiling by long chains, each place setting was white, from plates to napkins and to the single white flower beside each crystal goblet. A thousand young German men had filed in and taken their places. And now the invocation was about to begin.

Perhaps he had died, and now he was in heaven at the banquet of the elect. Stefan Blauer could almost have found such an explanation of his presence there believable after the unexpectedly grueling journey he'd just suffered.

At six A.M. as ordered, a black Mercedes-Benz limousine had arrived at the door of his apartment building to take him to his meeting with the SS. He had slept fitfully and awoken drawn and nervous. He had been furious with himself for his lack of nerve, but there were times when the body went its own way, or so it seemed, as it had that night, tortured by a demon made only more powerful by sleep. There was nothing to be done.

He had washed and shaved and put himself together

as best he could. But he was certain that in any mental duel the SS men would now have the upper hand.

As the car left his Beckmannstrasse address, the sight of the Preussen Park—still, hazy, a mass of purple-hued green in the early morning light—refreshed him as he sat alone in the great car except for the chauffeur behind a glass screen.

He had not expected to be making the trip alone, but had said nothing to the driver as the uniformed man held the door open for him, then crisply clapped it shut behind him. If traveling alone was intended to unnerve him (as it actually did under the circumstances), he would surprise them. He would savor this time alone, this time to think.

And he had, until the car had left Charlottenburg and taken the Autobahn to the west. He had tapped on the glass screen to notify the driver of a wrong turn, but the chauffeur paid no attention. Perhaps he was deaf, deaf and dumb like Byzantine eunuchs, thought Stefan, but this SS car was not taking him to the destination he had been told, not by this route.

Absurdly enough, he was being kidnapped. The idea had dawned on him slowly. When he tried the doors, he found them locked by some mechanism at the driver's seat. He struggled to control the natural panic rising in him. One could only hope to deal successfully with the SS by maintaining a show of strength.

He sank back into the upholstery and crossed his legs. He thought he caught the chauffeur grinning at him briefly in the rearview mirror. It seemed unreasonable that the SS were planning to liquidate him; what could be their reason for doing so? The chauffeur's all-too-human grin at his dilemma, plus this brief internal dialogue, had steeled his nerves.

It was then that he had noticed the speaking horn by which he could talk directly to the driver.

"This is not the route specified in my orders. Where

are you driving . . ." he had leaned forward to glimpse the chauffeur's shoulder insignia, "Sergeant," he concluded. As an army man, it galled Blauer to address an SS man by a military rank.

"Vogelsang, *mein Hauptmann*!"

Vogelsang. Stefan's head had swum for a minute. That was in the Rhineland. A good full day's journey, nonstop, from Berlin. This was madness. Why had he not been ordered to take a wagon-lit last night and save the waste of a full day?

Before he had formed the question, he already knew the answer: demoralization. He would arrive at Vogelsang exhausted and nervous. For a meal and a good night's rest, he would be putty in their hands. But for what reason? Surely this was not just a petty irritation contrived by the SS to further gall the Wehrmacht. No, there was a reason.

What was Vogelsang?

Stefan Blauer racked his brain for even a hint. What went on at Vogelsang? And then he remembered something: it was one of the Reich training centers. But for what he did not know. This sort of information was not common knowledge in Germany, and as an army officer, he had no reason to know. The Wehrmacht was not privy to the inner workings of the National Socialist Party.

Blauer had tried to interest himself in the scenery streaming past the motorcar, but it was too flat, too monotonous to provide much entertainment. The Autobahn successfully sidetracked any point of human congestion or geographical strain. As a highway system, it was total twentieth-century efficiency—and boring.

Precisely at noon the chauffeur had announced that a light luncheon could be found in a footlocker under the backseat. Blauer had found it and eaten gratefully.

The final ascent to the castle of Vogelsang had been a breathtaking journey up from the Rhine Valley, along winding roads bordering precipices full of mist and clouds, a setting worthy of the exploits of Siegfried. Vogelsang was all German legend and high romanticism.

"What is the meaning of this change of itinerary?" he had barked as he had gotten out of the limousine at Vogelsang and attempted to stretch his cramped limbs without being noticed.

"Forgive me, *mein Hauptmann*," the SS officer sent out to greet him had replied. "You will be briefed very shortly. May I show you to your quarters and then to the refectory? We dine at seven sharp . . . in . . ." The SS man checked his watch. "In twenty minutes. *Heil Hitler!*" He saluted.

The meal was plain, but good. The invocation had been too general—personal dedication to the ideals and goals of the Thousand Year Reich—to give Blauer more information about Vogelsang or his assignment. He had eaten with relish, as only a tired, hungry man does, at a guest table, where he was alone with an SS officer of surprising civility.

"Most impressive," Blauer had said at the close of the invocation, in hopes of glossing over the traditional army-SS animosity and of prodding his host into a spontaneous explanation of the purpose of Vogelsang.

"I hope you will find the local wine equally so," the man had suavely replied, filling Blauer's goblet, then toasting his health.

Stefan realized that the SS man was his match, far from the cloddish caricature Wehrmacht officers preferred painting of their rivals. Dinner conversation consisted of almost excruciatingly clever banter: Blauer learned nothing.

Simultaneously, in a smaller hall in the crypts of the castle, another evening meal was shared by the Reichsführer of the SS with his twelve superior officers. The meal was taken in silence. An invocation came at the end, but only after the table had been cleared and the servants gone.

"Gentlemen," began the Reichsführer, "in the most sacred of Aryan traditions, twelve of you are gathered here with your leader to decide on the merits of the candidate I have had brought to Vogelsang and who is waiting at this moment for our summons." The twelve men nodded or murmured their agreement. "Need I say that the candidate's quest will be crucial to the future of the Reich. So," he paused in emphasis, "let us be as one in our decision now as we are in our ancient race: One People, One Reich, One Führer!"

"*Heil Hitler,*" they uttered together. The shout echoed in the hall.

"Reichsführer," began a short-haired blond officer as he rose to his feet. The almost religious flicker of the candlelight which illuminated the small hall seemed to burnish the taut skin over his high cheekbones.

"Kriegshofer," acknowledged the Reichsführer.

"This man Blauer's suitability is based, in part, on the notes made by his father concerning his son's astrological destiny, is it not? Then, since we know Gerd Blauer to have been a traitor, why suppose his astrological interpretation to be any more reliable?"

From the differing reactions of the men present, it was immediately evident that they were split into two factions, and that they had been for some time. Kriegshofer had been and was still nominally in charge of the mission. He had to keep its power for himself, damn the cost.

Seated next to the Reichsführer was an older man with graying, wavy brown hair. He cleared his throat, breaking the tense silence of the room. Remaining seated as if to emphasize his seniority, he began to speak.

"And are the sins of the father visited on the son?"

"A point well taken, Sebottendorf," interrupted the Reichsführer solemnly. If there had been any doubt as to the nature of the group's decision, there was none any longer. Dissent would be temporarily tolerated, however, for a brief time. Kriegshofer's faction was still powerful enough to warrant that much respect.

"Come now, my dear Klaus," continued Sebottendorf, "the report has covered this point quite thoroughly. If I must recapitulate—Gerd Blauer was a firstrate astrologer. I knew the man: firstrate. His subsequent treason has nothing to do with his proficiency. All calculations and analyses were made at the son's birth and, need I point out, long before he lost sight . . ." He cleared his throat again. "Such a pity. Such a waste."

Insolently Kriegshofer did not allow for any silence to crown Sebottendorf's solemn statement of regret for a brother gone astray. He also failed to rise to his feet to speak.

"Young Blauer certainly has none of the elder's talent."

Sebottendorf reddened at Kriegshofer's impertinence.

"And I say, all the better. Your ignorance of the ideal qualities for such a candidate are embarrassingly apparent, Kriegshofer."

"Should I be embarrassed, sir?"

"Enough!" The Reichsführer brought the palm of his hand down flat on the table.

Sebottendorf gave a nod of thanks to the Reichsführer.

"Blauer is, shall we say, the perfect fool, the innocent, the pure one required for such a quest. He will be our Parsifal," added Sebottendorf in hushed tones.

"May I point out most respectfully," replied Kriegshofer immediately, "that Stefan Blauer can hardly be considered *pure* . . . and certainly not in National

Socialist terms, gentlemen." Kriegshofer closed his eyes
for a moment; a smirk of triumph played around his
mouth. "He *is* half-American." Kriegshofer's young
hard-liners did not bother to hide their amusement.
Everyone there knew that America was a racial pigsty.

The Reichsführer raised his hand. The table fell silent.

"Gentlemen, this is Vogelsang. Here we develop political and spiritual qualities for the future leadership
of the Reich. Let us be beyond such . . . such petty
power plays."

As Stefan Blauer followed his SS host down into
what appeared to be the depths of the castle of Vogelsang, the very massiveness of the masonry prompted
the remembrance of a theory his father had once re-
lated to him. Stefan must have been seven or eight
years old at the time.

It concerned the nature and purpose of the Great
Pyramid of Egypt. That great geometric construction
was no pharaoh's tomb; it was a temple of initiation.
Its corridors, its halls, its pits served as a microcosm of
the human fate, through which the candidate for the
priesthood must pass in order to be received into the
Brotherhood of Sacred Wisdom.

Stefan had loved his father. Like all other school-
boys he had learned that the pyramids were tombs.
Briefly he had wondered at his father's story, but with
a child's wisdom had said nothing. (Didn't his father
know he was too old for fairy tales?)

Gerd Blauer had pursued that Sacred Wisdom. Stefan liked to think that his father had died in heroic
pursuit of it. But, personally, his father's obsession had
held no appeal for him. Stefan preferred the concrete.
By instinct he was a man of action: a warrior.

Yet now his father's words held immediate reality

somehow. And this would not be the last time. Intuitively Stefan realized that when he had stepped into the Mercedes limousine that morning, his life had entered the realm of his father's.

Stefan decided to be blunt. He stopped dead in his tracks. His host turned around quizzically.

"What have I been brought here for?"

The SS man appraised Blauer quickly, then shook his head.

"Consider it an honor, Captain Blauer. Vogelsang is dedicated to the service of the Reich. It is . . ." He paused obviously to consider the choice of words. "It is only for the elite. Isn't that enough?"

"Should it be?"

"Yes, I think so. Come, or we shall be late."

Blauer followed in silence. His candidness had failed. Vogelsang was obviously not a place where candor was held in much esteem. Perhaps he had been foolish to try to pry his host for information. Then, he thought, mentally shrugging his shoulders, perhaps not. He had simply been true to his nature. He was a military man, not a . . . He laughed to himself: just what were the SS? The question made him shudder, because the SS existed, incontrovertibly; they were something concrete, and yet he knew nothing about them except the reality of their existence—black uniforms, death's-head insignia and all.

He had not counted on the SS when he had returned to serve the Reich in '33.

Stefan Blauer had only to wait a short time seated on a plain wooden bench in a small anteroom facing the two massive leaves of a great oaken door. His host had left him there alone.

"Stefan Blauer?" A tall, older man with graying, wavy hair held open one of the leaves of the great door. Stefan stood and saluted, despite not having been addressed by his military rank.

"Mein Herr!" Stefan in turn did not bother with the niceties of this uniformed SS man's rank. The man smiled: this subtlety had not gone unnoticed.

"My name is Sebottendorf. I was a friend of your father." Stefan was unable to hide his surprise. "Please come in."

As Blauer entered the room, the Reichsführer and all eleven SS officers turned to face him. Sebottendorf shut the door behind Stefan and resumed his seat next to the Leader. Blauer stood before the round table. No seat was offered him. He stood at attention but did not salute.

The Reichsführer rose slowly to his feet and gave the Nazi salute. Stefan followed suit. The Reichsführer sat down again. Still no seat was offered Blauer. He took it upon himself to stand at ease. He thought he caught a brief smile on the Reichsführer's mouth as he did this, but it was too gloomy in the candlelit hall to be sure.

The atmosphere of the place was like a sealed tomb. Behind the man who had saluted him was a great swastika banner in red, white and black. There was something ominous about this symbol, as it stood in this room, which Stefan had never felt before. He had never had much interest in politics; his job as an army officer did not require it. His duty was to serve the German government in power. The Third Reich had already accomplished much in Germany, and Blauer was enthusiastic about the future, but he did not feel it necessary to become overly involved in party politics.

Suddenly, however, in this room before these men he felt that his lack of political savvy made him vulnerable. He felt naïve, and for a reason he could not put his finger on.

The Reichsführer cleared his throat. "Hauptmann Stefan Blauer, welcome to Vogelsang."

"Thank you, sir."

"You are most probably wondering why you have been summoned here. I shall not keep you in suspense any longer. You have been selected by myself and these officers, as well as by the highest levels—the *very* highest levels—of the Reich, for a crucial assignment. Henceforth we shall refer to the mission by its code name: Phoenix.

"You know, I trust, something of the history of the German race, of its Aryan ancestry and of the great struggle for the universe in which we are engaged."

"I know what every German knows . . ."

"Your father did not discuss these matters with you in greater detail?" The Reichsführer's tone betrayed exasperation.

"No, sir." Blauer suddenly thought of the Great Pyramid. "Practically nothing at all."

"Pity! Did he ever tell you of the history of the Holy Grail?"

"The Holy Grail? I don't think my father did, sir. In school, of course—"

"You know what it is, however?" interrupted the Reichsführer.

"I believe, sir, that it is the mythical chalice of Christ used at the Last Supper. In the Middle Ages, according to legend, various knights went in search of . . ." Blauer paused. The Reichsführer looked impatient. Sebottendorf looked pained. The rest of the table either grinned, tight-lipped, or looked restless. "Wagner's *Parsifal* is based on this legend."

"Ah, you are familiar with the operas of Wagner," perked up the Reichsführer. "Good. Very good. Then let me come to the point: you are to be the Parsifal of the Third Reich."

There was a hush in the room. Blauer blinked. He had not quite understood. In the opera, Parsifal was the innocent, pure knight who eventually found and saved the Grail. But to refer to him as Parsifal—it made absolutely no sense. In any other circumstance he would have found the statement ludicrous.

"I'm afraid I don't quite understand," Stefan began.

The round table burst into laughter. Stefan grew visibly angry. "I don't think an officer of the Wehrmacht need be insulted by—" he shouted.

The Reichsführer raised his hand for calm. "Please do not misinterpret, Captain Blauer. It is simply that in your . . . in your ignorance you prove yourself the ideal choice."

"And again I protest this . . ." Stefan's apprehension, his fear of the SS, had turned to anger.

"Rest assured, Blauer, that in this case ignorance is a virtue. In no way are you being derided. Nor would we have brought you this great distance to insult the Wehrmacht. The time is quickly drawing near when all segments of the Reich must work as one man."

"If that is the case," began Blauer, still secure in his anger and in the conciliatory tone of the Reichsführer, "I believe I am owed a concrete explanation of why I have been brought here."

Sebottendorf rose slowly to his feet. All the eleven other members of the secret conclave, as well as the Reichsführer, gave him their undivided attention. If they had a spiritual father, these elite members of the SS gathered in that nearly airless room, then it was Sebottendorf. Sebottendorf had revealed to them all the value and the power of the Grail.

"The Grail, Stefan," began Sebottendorf in a fatherly way which was premeditated to throw Blauer off balance, "is the final link. The Jews have—or in fact no longer have—their Ark of the Covenant. While we, the pure descendants of the Aryans, implacable enemies of the defiling, murderous Jews, will soon— *through you*, my dear boy—have our Holy Grail back again. With it our link to the ancient past, to our forefathers, will be made secure. With it we shall vanquish the vile, black forces which have contaminated us, held us back from our destiny—we shall vanquish them once and for all."

The hushed respect in the room unnerved Blauer much more than Sebottendorf's paternalism. He did not know quite how to say what was immediately in his mind.

"*Mein Oberstgruppenführer,* this Grail . . . with all due respect, sir, it is only a myth and . . ."

"Ah, but my dear Stefan, it is not a myth. The Grail is real. It exists. And furthermore, we have good reason to believe you will know how to find it."

Stefan looked about the room for a second before refocusing his attention on Sebottendorf, who stood facing him across the table. Everyone in that room believed totally in what Sebottendorf was telling him.

They were all insane.

Blauer's mind raced for a strategy.

"If this Grail does exist—and I do not wish to contradict you, Herr Sebottendorf—I frankly cannot see what its concrete value is. Surely we are in the realm of . . . of symbolism."

Sebottendorf smiled slowly. How innocent, how nearly foolish young Blauer was. He stared at the young officer in silence for a moment. His inner pleasure was intense, almost orgasmic. Before him, before a high priest of the sacred knowledge as was Sebottendorf, stood the sacrificial lamb: the perfect fool. If he had ever really had any doubts as to Gerd Blauer's craft, they were gone now. Young Blauer was a full-blooded military man dedicated to German ideals. Furthermore, his obvious honesty, integrity and earnestness would make him trusted and believed. Stefan Blauer was fated to find the Grail. And he would find it for the Thousand Year Reich. History would never be the same again.

"Symbolism? Well, I do not want to go into the power of symbolism, as you call it, Stefan. Suffice it to say that it has power on the symbolic level. But the Grail also has, we thoroughly believe, real power in the form of knowledge, information. The Grail contains the key to mastery over the material universe. To put it more candidly, to make something out of seemingly nothing, to build castles in the air—to have everything mankind needs to make life again the life of the gods it once was."

"And the power to destroy cities, continents. To destroy our enemy, to bring the world to its knees," interjected Kriegshofer with precise solemnity.

It was Kriegshofer who jarred Blauer out of his disbelief.

"If you will, Kriegshofer," sighed Sebottendorf. "If you must put it this way, though it is hardly necessary. With the Grail the world will come to us."

"That is your opinion, Herr Sebottendorf." The young Kriegshofer's eyes had become slits. Blauer watched them, fascinated. It was the kind of fascination certain reptiles cast over their prey. He had to shake himself free of those eyes even though they were not directed at him but at the older man. He did it by speaking.

"Herr Sebottendorf, why do you think that I am the man for this assignment? I don't know anything about these matters. My father did, certainly, but I . . ."

"And your father is precisely the key." Sebottendorf turned immediately away from Kriegshofer to look elatedly at Blauer. "Your father himself selected you."

Blauer could not have been more stunned had a gun been shot at him point-blank. Anything was possible. He had not seen his father alive since August of '29. Why hadn't von Eschenberg—?

"Yes, it's true, Hauptmann Blauer. It is true."

Sebottendorf proceeded to relate to Blauer what everyone else in the hall already knew. Blauer had been fingered by fate, as it were, and his own father had made manifest that call from the Infinite. Stefan was incredulous. But it was not beyond his father.

Why had he never told his son? Why had it been left up to the SS?

"I'm sure," continued Sebottendorf, "your father would have told you about this . . . had it not been for his unfortunate accident."

"Yes, I'm sure he would have, had he . . ." Blauer allowed his voice to trail off as he scanned the men at the table. They knew a great deal more than they were telling him. His instincts told him so. And they were making him their pawn. "But I think that would have made all the difference in the world as to my qualifications." They were caught by surprise.

"How is that?" Sebottendorf's voice was stern. The older man was becoming exasperated. Blauer was not showing the fervor he had hoped for.

Blauer thought fast.

"Well, you must see that in telling me he also would have groomed me for the task. He would have told me things I would have to know to be successful. And, the fact is, he didn't. He was killed." His last statement echoed in the hall. It was as if an accusation had been levied.

These men had had something to do with his father's accident. They knew something. He looked from face to face; they all avoided him.

He was sure of it now.

A smirk of triumph passed over Kriegshofer's face.

"But that poses no problem," announced Sebottendorf.

"What?" Blauer had lost the thread of the conversation.

"We have such a mentor for you, my dear Stefan. A supremely eminent one. A Tibetan. His name is Ramyan Langsung. He will ride with you back to Berlin. You will have plenty of time to talk on the way."

"You seem unwilling to serve the Reich, Herr Blauer." Kriegshofer's voice interrupted like a whiplash.

"My life is devoted to service of the Reich. That is the sworn duty of a Wehrmacht officer, *mein Oberststurmführer*. Simply put, I don't see how a man as ignorant of these matters as I am can serve well in this case."

Kriegshofer smiled; his eyes narrowed. "I might tend to agree . . ."

"Fortunately, Blauer, that is not for you to decide. It has been decided for you." The Reichsführer brought an end to the debate. "Now then, your American ancestry will be of great help, I think."

"I am a German." Blauer was immediately on his guard.

"But your mother was American, was she not? You attended West Point. You do speak American English flawlessly, do you not? Then that is the point. You will make this search as an American. A perfect cover. We should not like our enemies to know of our search for the Phoenix Formula, now would we?"

Blauer looked puzzled for a second, then smiled. The Reichsführer continued. "You understand? I consider this term a more scientific approach. This is what disturbs you, if I'm not mistaken." The Reichsführer looked to the ceiling for a moment before going on. "With all due respect for Herr Doktor Sebottendorf's erudition . . ." he gave a nod in the man's direction, "we are really talking about a formula, a secret weapon, if you will, which we must have for two reasons: it is part of our patrimony as purified Germans, in pursuit of our ancient glory, and, second, if we do not seize it, others will." Then, as if in answer to Blauer's unspoken skepticism: "We know the Zionists are aware of it." There was no need to say more.

Until then Kriegshofer had remained silent. If there had been a hope that on seeing Blauer, they would reject him and leave the search in his own far more capable hands, those hopes were dashed. Blauer had enchanted most of them. His military bearing, his unflinching integrity and his practical qualifications for the mission excited their imagination. Now Kriegshofer would have to act alone. He would begin with a surprise.

"Hauptmann Blauer." The Reichsführer raised an eyebrow as Kriegshofer rose to his feet. "I congratulate you. I shall not hide from you the fact that this has been my mission up until now. I would prefer it to remain so. But I am not blind. I bow to your obvious qualifications . . ."

"Absolutely invisible to me, sir."

Kriegshofer smiled. "Your modesty is commendable, Captain. Still I would like to make a suggestion to the council. I believe, Blauer, that you are acquainted with an American girl, Kitty Hammersmith." Blauer flushed visibly. Kriegshofer smiled and raised his hand. "And why not, Captain? She is beautiful, I hear. My suggestion, gentlemen, is that Blauer and Miss Hammersmith travel together as . . . as newlyweds. A perfect cover."

There were exclamations of surprise in the room. The brow of the Reichsführer furrowed in thought.

"Don't you think the mission is too delicate?. She would have to know why . . ." Blauer voiced his objections tentatively.

"Why would she need to know, Blauer? I think you can find it in you to place it all on the level of sheer romance: travel, mountains . . ." Kriegshofer's smile stopped Blauer. "You have quite a reputation for romance, Captain, do you not?"

The Reichsführer interrupted. "Kriegshofer, you are out of order." The SS officer bowed and sat down. There was a pause. "We shall consider the idea later . . . in private."

Blauer noted a smile creep over Kriegshofer's face, then vanish. He couldn't fathom the man's motives.

"Reichsführer, I cannot be sure that Miss Hammersmith would agree."

"Quite so, Blauer. But we'll decide the matter later. Do you accept your assignment?"

"All I need sir, is a signed order from the Wehrmacht freeing me for an SS mission."

The Reichsführer smiled and reached into a folder on the table in front of him.

"Your orders, Steven Blauer," he said in English.

"I suppose you have a motive, Kriegshofer." Häger paced the floor of the small anteroom. "I would never have thought you would give up control so easily."

Kriegshofer got up from the great leather and wood campaign chair and crushed his cigarette under his brilliantly polished boot. His lean face creased in a smile.

Häger averted his gaze. He did not like to meet that smile face on. Though they were equals in rank in the *Schutzstaffel*, the elite corps known rakishly as SS, Kriegshofer's sheer will to power made him superior. Häger preferred to think of the difference between them as one of appearance; Kriegshofer looked the perfect SS man: tall, tensely muscular and blond, he was riveting in his black uniform with its silver death's-head insignia. Häger's character was equally quick and commendably sly and he was dedicated to the Reich, but he just did not cut the same figure. He was shorter and definitely on the stocky side.

"A clever man knows when to change tactics, Häger." Now Kriegshofer began to pace while Häger stood still, his hands behind his back, contemplating the chair just vacated but not sitting down in it. "What if I should tell you that Blauer's mentor, his so-called uncle, the Count von Eschenberg, is a homosexual?"

"You aren't serious, Kriegshofer. This is a well-known secret. I dare say it is one of the reasons behind the Reichsführer's confidence in Blauer. A nice point of blackmail. Dear old Uncle Hans's life for—"

"*And* that Miss Hammersmith is a Zionist agent."

"What?"

"I think you heard me, Häger. Your ears are known to be highly sensitive."

"You must reveal this in the—"

"Don't be absurd, Häger." Kriegshofer stopped pacing and stood staring at him impatiently.

Suddenly Häger looked up and met Kriegshofer's eye with a grin of satisfaction. "Brilliant, *mein Oberstgruppenführer!* The mission is ours once again!"

There was a knock on the door and a *Sturmmann* entered and saluted. They both returned his salute.

"The council will reconvene immediately, sirs." The SS private first class opened the door wide for the two SS generals.

"Thank you, Private," replied Kriegshofer.

Chapter Four

Ramyan Langsung paused after relating the details of the massacre of the Cathari in 1244. The limousine was entering the outskirts of Potsdam. It was only a short ride now to Berlin and Charlottenburg. Stefan Blauer was looking forward to shutting the door of his flat behind him and forgetting about the Phoenix mission for a while.

And then he thought of Kitty. What an odd twist that had been. But the Reichsführer seemingly had conceded to Kriegshofer's experience in the Grail matter. It would be up to Blauer, however, to convince her.

He focused his attention back to the Lama's words. It was also up to him to learn quickly and to succeed where Kriegshofer had failed. A point of honor. But he had sensed a veiled threat to himself, as well as the open one to von Eschenberg, from Kriegshofer.

"The Grail has not been seen in the West since that time." Ramyan Langsung spoke only English.

"And in the East?"

The Lama smiled in response.

"You might now ask, Mr. Blauer, what the Grail looks like, what it really is. Some Western legends have it that it is the Christ's chalice from the Last Supper. But no, no, Mr. Blauer. Look for something much more ancient. Perhaps a set of tablets? The Philosopher's Stone? Also a legend, but much more likely to be the truth under the Veil. Much truth in the world has had to be veiled. Still must be veiled . . .

"He who possesses the Grail, possesses mighty knowledge from the past—dangerous knowledge if in the wrong hands. But I think, Mr. Blauer, that your hands are the right hands. I see this in you."

Blauer could only smile. The man sounded like a gypsy fortune-teller. The elderly Tibetan monk looked embarrassingly like a tramp, with an old overcoat over his saffron-colored robes. Stefan had expected a more resplendent personage. But he did feel what could be described as an aura of sanctity around this shaven-headed little man with Oriental features and almost leathery, taut, matte skin which added a certain reptilian quality to his appearance. Sebottendorf had introduced them, which made Stefan wonder whether Kriegshofer had ever had the benefit of the Lama's advice.

"And Kriegshofer?" asked Blauer point-blank.

"I have not had the pleasure." The monk smiled in an opaque, Oriental fashion, which said nothing.

"So, Mr. Blauer, I would humbly suggest beginning your search at Montségur." The monk emphasized his suggestion by tapping Blauer's knee. A kindly smile spread across his face. "The mountains of the Languedoc are quite beautiful in the month of June. The perfect setting for a honeymoon, what?" Blauer smiled at the monk's British turn of phrase.

"Languedoc—that's the south of France, isn't it?"

"And the ancient stronghold of the Cathari." But his attention was diverted elsewhere. The Lama looked sharply out the window of the moving car. Then with his ivory-headed cane he knocked on the window isolating them from the driver. The limousine drew to a halt beside the curb. Ramyan Langsung turned toward the surprised Blauer with an impish glint in his eye.

"Well, good-bye now, Steven Blauer. I shall catch a train here." He raised a hand to silence Blauer. "I prefer being on my own. We shall surely meet again another day, I think."

Before Stefan could reply, the driver had already come around and opened the door for the elderly Tibetan. With surprising agility the Lama got out of the car, turned for a second to wave good-bye, then vanished into the determined crowd heading into the train station after a day's work.

As the limousine sped on up to Berlin in the fast-falling dusk, Stefan sorted out the events of the past twenty-four hours for the hundredth time.

The Phoenix Formula. A mythical bird rising from the ashes. Yes, but whose ashes, really? There had seemed to be two points of view: Blauer was deeply disturbed by Kriegshofer's.

And then, when Stefan had suggested turning to von Eschenberg, as a close confidant of his father, for information as well as to the Tibetan, a sinister humor had run around the table. "By all means, Blauer." It had been Kriegshofer, grinning, who had broken the silence. "Perhaps this way you might manage to give some value to the poor life of a pervert."

This official and crude declaration of Hans's homosexuality had shaken Blauer. Not because it came as a surprise: he had always known, since he was old enough to know such things. And he had been raised to think nothing of it. But now in Germany there were the new laws. A homosexual was worse than a Jew.

Blauer glanced out the window to distract himself: he had begun to feel fear. Kriegshofer had not been subtle. Von Eschenberg was the only person left whom Stefan could call family. Blauer's success on his mission would keep Hans alive. Failure—and something about Kriegshofer's manner had assumed his failure—would insure "enforcement of the law."

As the limousine sped into the Charlottenburg section of Berlin, his imagination, given time to wander, had unearthed a new source of worry. What were the true motives of the SS in suggesting that Kitty go along with him? A fresh object of blackmail? But then reason reasserted itself. There were no grounds for blackmail.

The car pulled to a stop in front of his building. Blauer opened the door himself, motioning to the driver to stay put, and got out, slamming the door shut. As the concierge greeted him, asking if he had had a pleasant trip, the limousine pulled away.

As he rode up in the elevator, Blauer made the decision to call and then go over to von Eschenberg's place immediately. Seeing him would perhaps dissipate his fears for him. And he wanted to find out what Hans knew about his father's plans for him and the Grail.

But by the time he had turned the key in his door, he had changed his mind. There was not much point in doing that now. As he had thought of how he would phrase his questions to Hans, he had realized suddenly that he was not so much interested in what von Eschenberg knew of the Grail and his father as he was in venting his anger with him for being a source of blackmail. There was no point to that at all.

Blauer went into his bedroom and began taking off his uniform. What he needed then and there was a good, hot bath. It would relax him. And then he would call Kitty Hammersmith. A much more pleasant idea, and it was time for his reward of pleasure. He was almost positive that she was in love with him.

Kitty Hammersmith glanced at the delicately small wristwatch she always wore, then looked back out the window of her suite at the Hotel Monbijou. The traffic on the Damm below was sparse. In the twilight the river Spree had taken on a gunmetal, mirrorlike quality as it inched its narrow, serpentine way through the heart of Berlin.

She opened the french doors and stepped out onto the balcony.

She had not expected to hear from Stefan so soon. It had been less than forty-eight hours since she had seen him last. Supposedly in the interim he had been away on assignment. She knew only too well what the assignment was about. Of course she had given him no inkling of what she knew. She had sensed that he was nervous about it, so she had suspected that she knew more about what he was in store for than he did himself. The unknown coming from the SS would shake up even a Wehrmacht officer.

Actually that eve of his journey he had seemed to abandon his tension, losing himself in the enjoyment of seeing her again after all those years. She had been pleased to note that his memory of their previous encounter was nearly photographic. How she had looked. How she had thought (or how he thought she had thought). And then one thing had led to another. A bottle of good wine with an excellent supper in a fashionable bistro. A growing closeness. And then the inevitable. He had suggested going back to his flat for a nightcap. And, after a demure pause, she had accepted.

Kitty smiled to herself now. She honestly liked Stefan. And being able somehow to separate the man from his Wehrmacht role, her affection would come across to him as totally genuine. He was such a romantic. She was convinced that he was in love with her. At his place he had fixed two drinks, turned on the radio, turned off the lights, then danced with her in the dark.

After they had made love, it had been she who had

suggested that she go back to her hotel so that he could get a good night's sleep for what was left of the night.

Poor Stefan. He must have been exhausted in the morning. She knew he had been up at dawn.

And now his surprising telephone call. He had dressed his request to take her to dinner in the trappings of passionate romance (he had thought of nothing but her while he had been away), but she had sensed a more rational urgency underneath.

She hoped that whatever seemed to have precipitated events was positive.

She lit a cigarette, then put it out after a couple of drags. In any case she could only be glad things were moving ahead rapidly. She found Berlin alone depressing.

Her suite was located on the tenth floor, high enough up to be able to see past the Spree and over the southern half of the city. The streets were not visible, but the buildings were. The more baroque-looking theaters on Unter den Linden, then further on the Wilhelmstrasse the chancelleries of the Third Reich, monolithic, square-columned and draped in towering swastika banners.

An inadvertent shudder overtook her.

She glanced down to the street below in time to see Stefan Blauer get out of a taxi and stride into the hotel. She walked back into the sitting room and shut the french doors behind her. Despite the lateness of sunset in June this far north, the evening breezes over the city became quite chilly.

Blauer had put on civilian evening dress to go out that night. The change, the shedding of his military self, had refreshed him despite the strain of the past forty-eight hours. Belatedly now he wondered if his fatigue showed.

"Can I mix you a cocktail, Stefan?"

He could not take his eyes off Kitty. In her pale jade-green evening gown she looked like a goddess. He made her feel a bit self-conscious. She had moved toward the dry bar set up against one wall of the sitting room before he could reply.

"I'd love a dry martini." He got up and followed her partway across the room. "And you really should start learning to call me Steven."

Kitty laughed, a puzzled expression on her face. "You haven't switched nationalities on me, have you?"

"Not exactly." With amusement he watched her expression change.

Kitty put down the bottle of dry vermouth without using it. "Oh? That's an enigmatic reply." She stood waiting for him to go on, but he hesitated. For the first time she noticed that he looked exhausted. When he had called that evening, he had sounded almost out of breath.

"Kitty, how would you like to go off on a trip with me?"

Kitty began to laugh; not in her wildest imagination had she expected this.

Blauer smiled. He relished her surprise. "It's no joke."

Kitty moved quickly to remedy things: she couldn't have hoped for a more perfect suggestion.

"I'm sorry, Stef . . . Steven. It's just so unexpected."

"Do you always laugh at the unexpected?"

"Very American of me, I guess?"

"I suppose it is. I'm not . . . not quite up on American mores. And that's where your traveling with me would be a distinct help." He was finding it hard to explain his proposal to her. Although the Reichsführer himself had suggested taking her along, it was left up to Blauer to judge how much to tell her.

"My orders are," he began slowly, "to travel as an American."

"Is this some cloak-and-dagger thing? I've always wanted to be Mata Hari."

He laughed with relief. She would make the whole arcane assignment bearable; she was doing so already.

"No, nothing like that really. No spying involved. Just a reconnaissance mission, so to speak. And my orders are to travel as an American, to make things easier."

"The Third Reich isn't exactly well loved in all quarters, is it?" Her quip surprised and annoyed him. But he did not want to get into politics now. What foreigners felt about the government was of little interest to him. It was the government that he was sworn to serve. Where were they all when the population of Berlin was near starvation in the twenties?

"I suppose you're right." His reply was deliberately laconic.

"Well, Steven, let me get you that martini." She began mixing a pitcher of them. He found himself eyeing her hungrily. Besides her spirit, her wit, she was enormously desirable to him. She made it difficult for him to keep in control of himself by her physical presence alone. Perhaps Helga had been right: he was quite the animal.

He walked up behind her at the dry bar. Trembling, he put his hand on her bare shoulder. She turned around slowly, her face tilted gently up toward his. He realized that he had never looked a woman in the eyes the way she drew him into hers. All artifice, all awkwardness vanished. He kissed her deeply on the mouth.

The mixing of martinis was forgotten as, their lips still pressed together, she turned to face him. He caught her up in his arms. The lust inside him broke free of the decorum he had felt obliged to obey out of respect for her. In minutes he was making love as lustily and freely as he would have to Helga or any other of the numberless Helgas who had passed through his life. But with one enormous, awesome difference for him: he was in love with Kitty Hammersmith.

Silently they went into her bedroom and undressed. They were like sleepwalkers. The silence of it all, her beauty as her gown slipped off her body, overwhelmed him.

In bed as he entered her he groaned deeply both with the sexual satisfaction of feeling himself inside her body and with a sense of completion, of safety in their communion. Kitty dug her fingernails into his broad back as she came within seconds after he did. He was a stupendous lover, she thought with disconcerting clarity as he lay panting on top of her, still throbbing inside her. But his ardor, his trust in her, was more than she had bargained on.

And then he was whispering into her ear: "You'll come with me then?" The piercing blue of his eyes held her fixed. She smiled and nodded.

Old Fritzl stood at attention, his hands folded behind his back as Hans von Eschenberg made his inspection of the dining room. The place settings for three were, of course, impeccable, from crystal to china to the correct array of silver needed to proceed through the five courses, which would begin to parade before them precisely at eight o'clock. Von Eschenberg glanced at his pocket watch, then slipped it on its gold chain back into the pocket of his waistcoat. It was approaching seven. Stefan and the American girl would be ringing the bell of the flat shortly.

"Very good, Fritzl. The claret is uncorked?"

"Yes, *mein Herr Graf*." The old family retainer became even more stooped and wizened-looking as he bowed to the Count von Eschenberg. A hint of a smile crossed Hans's face. He supposed that to modern Germans, to the young of the Third Reich, he must appear to be just as much an anachronism as old Fritzl.

"That will be all then, Fritzl." Von Eschenberg walked slowly out of the formal dining room, which in its classic French decor lay somewhere out of time, out of space, in a genteel world where form and detail mattered most, where life was a continual exercise in good manners, civilization and effortlessness.

He paused for a second before the tall, ornately framed mirror over the marble fireplace of the salon. He adjusted the spread of the wings of the white tie of his evening clothes—another formalistic, unnecessary gesture, he thought with the irony he entertained more and more. "Given the right series of events . . . a war . . ." he intoned aloud in the empty room. He and his kind would never survive a war. They would become so much dross, excess baggage from a past which it would then be very convenient, expedient, to dispense with.

Hans von Eschenberg did not bother to suppress a short laugh. He no longer felt embarrassed by the new morbidity of his sense of humor. He shrugged his shoulders at the impeccably distinguished-looking antique of a man reflected in the mirror. It was obvious that such a creature, an aristocrat parading in stately fashion across the plateau of his late fifties, was dispensable. And good riddance. His pace was grossly out of step with the times. Not to mention certain of his vices . . .

"*Ah, les vices* . . ." he spoke gently to the figure in the mirror. He shook his head in comic despair. They were good enough for ancient Greece and Rome, but for the New Age . . . really!

The doorbell sounded. Fritzl padded silently behind the figure of the aristocrat in the mirror and vanished beyond the other side of the gilt frame. The double doors of the salon opened and shut behind him. Fritzl vanished down the entry hall. In a few seconds he would open the door. And the evening would begin.

Stefan had been a serious child, preferring the company of his father and other adults to that of boys his own age. On weekends at the von Eschenberg estate he had occasionally been embarrassingly underfoot, trailing after his father like a dog weaned too early. And so he had been, from an American mother who, from Gerd Blauer's description, was much too caught up in the fevers of the Jazz Age to find it unnatural for her only son to be bundled off to Germany with his father after their divorce. When Gerd had suggested the possibility, she had seemingly leaped at the plan with gratitude as if offered immortality. She was spared motherhood, but the automobile had caught up with her in a fashionable, flapper's auto accident, which had in turn spared her the cold morning-after of the Crash in '29.

Poor child, Hans had thought, as he trailed after Gerd and himself on one of their philosophical walks through the tidy little forest on the southern border of the family land. The child haunted them, his presence an unpleasant reminder to Hans of Gerd's past, of the possibility that he might once again revert to female company for his pleasure. And then one day he could stand Stefan's presence no longer and insisted that the boy stay behind and play with the caretaker's children. Stefan had cried. His father had reprimanded him. Immediately the boy had dried his tears and marched off toward the gatehouse at the end of the drive to obey his father. Watching his small figure grow ever smaller as he proceeded down the drive, Hans had not felt so much pity or remorse at his selfish desire to have Gerd all to himself, as amazement at the boy's ability to turn off his tears when they were obviously useless and face up to his fate—something Hans himself had always found immensely difficult.

He heard Stefan's voice in the hall, but not that of the American girl. Von Eschenberg would have much preferred dinner alone with Stefan. They had only spoken once since his return from the meeting with the SS, and then on the telephone when Stefan had called to ask whether he might bring this girl around. They both suspected his telephone was tapped. Discussion of the SS meeting would have to wait.

When Hans heard her voice, clear, steady, thanking Fritzl in impeccable German, he thought it seemed a remarkable improvement over the usual run of Stefan's women. Von Eschenberg found suddenly that he was curious to meet her, and now that she was at his door, even eager. For a split second he was also a bit panicked, until he quickly mastered the strong vein of shyness masked for the world at large by his urbanity.

The door opened. Fritzl ushered the couple into the salon and von Eschenberg turned with a smile to greet them. Fritzl shut the double doors of the salon behind them, vanishing into the hall.

Stefan, too, seemed to hesitate for a split second as the door shut behind him. In that instant he decided there was no need to confront von Eschenberg with any of the ramifications of the Phoenix mission. What good would it do? Relieved, Stefan stepped forward with a smile, Kitty's hand on his arm.

The two men shook hands.

"Sir, may I present Miss Kitty Hammersmith from New York?" Stefan stepped back, Kitty forward, extending her hand. She seemed genuinely pleased to meet him, Hans thought, taking his hand.

"Welcome to Berlin, my dear."

"Thank you, Herr von Eschenberg." She gave a slight, very proper curtsy, due his rank. He was impressed. Kitty sensed it immediately and felt relieved. He seemed kind, a formal gentleman of the old school, but radiating warmth. Immediately she decided that she liked him. Kitty had great faith in her first impressions; they had never let her down.

"So," beamed von Eschenberg from one to the other,

"I thought we might start with a bit of champagne. A weakness of mine, I'm afraid. Do you care for champagne, Miss Hammersmith?" Hans had launched into English with gusto. He delighted in the lighthearted theatricality of upper-class British English.

"I adore it, sir." She hoped he didn't think her overly effusive. But von Eschenberg laughed as the double doors opened and Fritzl appeared, wheeling in a cart with champagne on ice and a tray of hors d'oeuvres.

"Come, my dear, let's sit down. Stefan?" He ushered them to the sofa nearest the fireplace and himself sat down in a great winged armchair facing the couple. Fritzl popped the cork and filled three glasses placed on a small silver tray. "That will be all, Fritzl," pronounced von Eschenberg in German. Fritzl bowed and left the salon. "A toast then? Stefan, will you do the honors?"

A wry grin flashed across Stefan's face.

"May I? To my fiancée, Miss Kitty Hammersmith, if we have your blessing, sir." The lie of their engagement struck the air like a whiplash.

"Why . . ." Stefan had never seen von Eschenberg so flustered. His normally pale complexion flushed in shock. Then he laughed. It was high, light, somewhat hysterical.

Instantly Stefan realized that he had insulted Hans by his cavalier engagement announcement. Something inside wanted to wound, to punish von Eschenberg for being a source of blackmail. He had never once before shown von Eschenberg the slightest disrespect. His sexual proclivities had never before been a problem to him. Now the SS had succeeded in making von Eschenberg just that: a burden, a limitation on his freedom, a source of blatant blackmail. And this was how he was showing his resentment.

"Then let us drink to that, and to your future happiness, both of you." Von Eschenberg raised his glass.

Stefan started to speak, to explain, but von Eschenberg's imperious solemnity silenced him. Stefan raised his glass. Confused, Kitty raised hers. She gave Stefan a quizzical look. She sensed something brutal in Stefan's gesture. Why didn't he explain further, about the mission, about his cover?

The three of them drank. The two men drained their glasses. Kitty put hers down after one sip.

"I think Stefan has some explaining to do," she said abruptly.

"Indeed?" said von Eschenberg, reaching over and pulling the bottle out of the silver ice bucket. He refilled Stefan's, then his own glass, after gesturing toward Kitty's. She shook her head.

Stefan was shaken by von Eschenberg's capacity to accept seeming betrayal in such a stoic fashion. It cast a new, dramatic light on the cruelties a homosexual had to bear to survive.

"Yes, I do, sir. We aren't really engaged . . ." he began lamely. Stefan felt intense shame.

Von Eschenberg sat back in the winged chair and took a sip, waiting serenely. Kitty watched first one, then the other. Though they were not father and son, she sensed nevertheless similarities and conflicts fathers and sons have with one another. At first she found it unnerving, then fascinating.

She knew nothing of von Eschenberg's private life, his vulnerability. She was puzzled. It did not seem to be the right way to treat someone who had been referred to as the only family Stefan had left.

Stefan began again. "It all has to do with my latest assignment."

Von Eschenberg smiled. "I take it your meeting with the SS went well."

"I suppose you could say that." Stefan shot von Eschenberg a shrewd glance. He wondered now how much the older man knew and whom he knew it from.

But von Eschenberg had a way of finding out as much as possible by seeming to know it all anyway.

"The SS gave you an assignment, I take it, then. I should say it was of the greatest importance. The Wehrmacht, my dear Miss Hammersmith, in case you didn't know what all Germany knows," he began, leaning forward toward Kitty, "entertains sentiments of great rivalry with the SS. Isn't this so, Stefan?"

Stefan cleared his throat. "That hardly matters, in this case." He considered von Eschenberg's remarks in front of a foreigner, even if it was Kitty, to be inappropriate.

"Your father was on assignment for the SS, Stefan, when he died. You knew that, didn't you?" An academic, offhanded smile sat on his face as he watched Stefan's face lose its composure. So the boy didn't know—or did he now?

"Yes . . . so I learned. Why hadn't you told me?"

"Oh, it hardly seemed important." Von Eschenberg's smile broadened slightly as if gaining territory. "And Miss Hammersmith has agreed to act as your fiancée in a—how to put it—a reconnaissance mission. I'm terribly curious, Miss Hammersmith, and forgive me if I am too prying, but why have you agreed? Am I honored to make the acquaintance of a member of the famous German-American Bund?"

Kitty laughed easily. Stefan glanced at her with surprise; he considered the question quite serious. She was delighted it had come; she had counted on it, planned for it. Her reply was spoken with the aplomb of a first-rate actor who knows the play well. "Frankly, Count von Eschenberg, I can't say I am a member, but I do have my sympathies. And then I think traveling with Stefan would be exciting. Don't you agree, Count?"

"I'm afraid Kitty is not politically committed," Stefan interrupted her.

"And why should she be, Stefan? Miss Hammersmith is American."

"Yes, we Americans are political simpletons. Frankly, sir, I find politics more and more of a bore. I'm taking after my mother after all."

Stefan listened with interest. They had not really discussed politics since they had met. But her presence in Berlin had seemed sympathetic enough. And then there was the way they had met in the first place.

"You know, Miss Hammersmith, that Stefan is half-American." Von Eschenberg smiled at his own innuendo: he did consider Stefan politically naïve.

"He confessed it to me at our first meeting in New York." She noted the count's surprise. "His mother's side, it seems. Of course, if she had been a Jew, he'd be a lot worse off, wouldn't he?" Von Eschenberg guffawed at Kitty's brazenness. Stefan looked appalled. He found her humor macabre, in poor taste. But he let it pass, mainly because von Eschenberg was laughing. The poor start to the evening was past, and he was pleased that they had taken a liking to each other. As pleased, he noted quietly for his own amusement, as if Kitty were in fact his fiancée. And then, to his surprise, he realized that nothing would make him happier.

Hans knew that Ramyan Langsung was not alone in Berlin. He was part of a small mission of Tibetans lodged as inconspicuously as possible in the embassy district off Tiergartenstrasse. Yet it always seemed to von Eschenberg as if the monk appeared out of thin air. This time the meeting had been preceded by a brief telephone call: the Lama had not identified himself on the phone and von Eschenberg had been quick enough not to identify him either. Hans had been aware for some time that they were keeping an eye on who entered and left his Charlottenburg residence. He had not been sure before that they had his telephone line under surveillance. The Lama's behavior, however, convinced him. Ramyan Langsung knew a great deal. It made him chuckle now at their paranoia, their stupidity: did they really think he knew that much? But later it had dawned on him: they were undoubtedly amassing evidence for his eventual liquidation. The Graf von Eschenberg could not simply disappear one night like some Jewish shopkeeper.

Hans waited now at the rendezvous, in front of the tiger cages in the Tiergarten at two in the afternoon. He looked at his watch, then sighed. What difference did the time make? No one cared. It was depressingly uneventful for von Eschenberg to absent himself from his small office in the Ministry of Culture for the remainder of the afternoon. Although it had not been quite so easy to shake off the man tailing him; it had taken a streetcar, then a taxi.

The almost soundless pacing of the great, long-muscled animals, the brutal, carnivorous odor from the cages, struck von Eschenberg as an ironically suitable setting for their meeting. Perhaps the Lama wanted him to contemplate this metaphor for his life, this symbol of the latent violence surrounding him. And then Ramyan Langsung appeared, meticulously well dressed in a suit, his hat shading his eyes just enough to make his identification as an Oriental difficult. After all, there were many Germans with the eyes of the Tartar.

The monk broke the silence: "Perhaps it will be recorded that you have met a lover before the tiger's cage." There was a touch of pity in the monk's voice. For a moment von Eschenberg felt the depth of his despair.

"Wouldn't you call it my karma?"

"No doubt, my dear Count." Ramyan Langsung turned to watch the tigers. His attention seemed intense, focusing on the power of the animals, their grace, their restlessness. After a pause he continued, speaking softly in English, his gaze still riveted to the movements of the tigers. "The time has come for Stefan. They are taking the risk. They believe now they cannot find it without him."

"Goddamn the Grail to hell!" Von Eschenberg had not raised his voice, however.

"It will not be as it was for his father."

"What is the guarantee?"

"But you speak so easily of karma." As if on cue, one of the tigers roared; the others followed. They ceased as abruptly as they had begun. "And now another thing. It is foolish not to respect what you love."

The monk had taken him by surprise. He found himself blurting out: "An old man's lust?" He winced. So they had undermined his self-respect that much. "Thank you. I will remember."

"You know better. The heart of it is love. Remember. And cherish the memory of Gerd Blauer." Von Eschenberg was moved to silence. For a few moments he experienced a lifting of the death sentence which he felt hanging over him, the knowledge of which he had learned to numb in the late evening with cognac. Tears now rushed to his eyes. And then the vision of salvation was gone.

"What about the American girl?" His whisper was hoarse from the sudden rush of emotion just past.

"She will help him."

"She is not a spy? Oh, Zionist or for the SS, it hardly matters. But come now . . ."

Ramyan Langsung turned to face von Eschenberg. The token of his calling, the maddeningly serene smile, was the extent of his reply to the accusation. And then he said: "It will not be long for you, my good and dear friend. Patience. Trust in God." He touched the brim of his hat, and before von Eschenberg could utter cynically, "Which God?" he was walking away.

Von Eschenberg winced from the silent reprimand like a chastened schoolboy. But as he left the zoo, he felt an inner relief.

By three P.M. he was home and seated in the English-leather armchair in his study. He hadn't had the stamina to return to his office. Something about the meeting had exhausted him: perhaps he would go upstairs and lie down. He was about to ring for Fritzl when he heard the bell of the front door. The old family retainer was padding his way to the door before von Eschenberg could issue a contrary order. He was expecting no one. His heart seemed to stop beating.

But seconds later from the hallway he heard the sound of a young woman's voice. Fritzl moved down the hall to the door of the study, opened it and shut the door behind him.

"It's that young American girl, *mein Herr Graf, Das Fräulein Hammerschmidt.*" Von Eschenberg smiled at Fritzl's Germanization of Kitty's family name. There was a trace of contempt in the voice of the old snob: he did not care much for women, much less for commoners.

"Show her in, Fritzl." The old servant clucked his disapproval and left to show her to the study. Von Eschenberg couldn't imagine what she wanted. He still clung to the notion that she was a spy, and, now that he thought about it, the Tibetan had not disclaimed this.

He stood up as she came into the room.

"I just thought I'd drop by and have a chat," she said cheerily. The dinner party had ended well, they had decided to like each other, and now her ebullient familiarity—so American, he thought—did not surprise him.

"Would you care for some tea?" He motioned her to a chair and went to ring for Fritzl.

"No, no, I can't stay long. And I'm not crazy about tea, if you must know." Von Eschenberg laughed.

"I do think it too early for a cocktail, don't you?"

"A bit, yes . . ."

"Now then . . . to what do I owe the pleasure—not that you need to have a specific reason."

She cleared her throat. "But I suppose I should . . . have a reason, that is. Oh, I thought maybe you and I could have a talk about Stefan." She sounded suddenly a bit flustered, he thought. He had been too gruff; he liked the girl.

"That is a subject we do have in common."

"I'm in love with him, you know."

"I never had the slightest notion that you were not, my dear Kitty. I would . . ."

She laughed. "Hardly expect a girl to run off on a trip with a man unless she had stars in her eyes?"

"Something like that." He raised an eyebrow. "Of course for a second it had crossed my mind that you just might be some kind of an adventuress."

She laughed deliciously. "And maybe I am. But not for money, Count. I have more than enough of that." He nodded at that. He believed her. He could tell money. She paused for a second. "This assignment of his, it's rather cutthroat, isn't it?"

"I don't know much about it, now, do I?"

"I can't believe that. Why are they letting me travel with him?"

"Odd one, that, I must agree. Of course, that way he could travel more convincingly as an American himself. Isn't that what Stefan said?"

"And what does Stefan think?"

"Frankly, I think he's in love with you and snatched at the opportunity. How about you, my dear Kitty?"

"I told you already that I love him . . ."

"Yes, and I might be inclined to believe that. But surely you're a spy."

The silence in the oak-paneled study became absolute; he listened calmly to the ticking of the clock, a souvenir of Zurich, of the Alps, of his youth in simpler times. Kitty began to laugh, then suddenly stopped.

"I'm afraid that's absurd; but what if I were—why would you care?"

"Only for Stefan's safety. I frankly don't give a fig about much else." His own candor surprised him; not only did he like Kitty, but for some strange reason he trusted her as well.

"Well," she laughed again, nervously, her hands resting in her lap, her eyes staring at them. "I'm not a spy. And from my wealth it should be easy to deduce that I'm hardly a Red." She looked up and fixed her eyes on von Eschenberg. "I can guarantee that on my honor. No harm will ever come from me." Her stare gripped him, forcing him to believe her.

"Then I won't worry anymore about it."

Silence followed, the ticking of the clock, then Kitty burst into laughter again.

"So you really do believe I'm a spy."

"I believe . . . what do I believe in this year of our Lord nineteen hundred and thirty-nine? I believe that you will knowingly do Stefan no harm."

"Nothing more than that?" Her eyes twinkled now with pleasure. Her high spirits were contagious. Small wonder Stefan was in love with her, he thought. And there was something else about her which made him pause, consider, then place his trust in her once more.

"I believe that you should attend the Festival at Bayreuth. Do you know about it? The Wagner pieces, epics, hymns to the German spirit. And there is one opera which you must *know*, must see above all, Kitty. It is *Parsifal*." She looked puzzled. The maddeningly serene smile of Ramyan Langsung had appeared on von Eschenberg's face.

"When is it to be put on?"

"I could get you the best seats, Kitty. For you and for Stefan—though he is barely interested in opera. I might add that this ability—to get you opera seats—is the extent—the full extent—of my power in Germany." As he spoke, he had sat up in his chair. He now seemed very tall, willful, angry. If, in fact, he was the typical dissolute aristocrat, he bore no trace of it at that moment. He was a very handsome man, she noticed suddenly.

"When? When is it?"

Von Eschenberg laughed. "Oh, my dear Kitty, in fact you won't get the chance, not this season."

"Why?"

"Will you promise me you will look it up, read the scenario at least?"

"Why won't I get a chance to see it?"

"Because you'll be traveling, my dear Kitty, traveling, both of you." He sank back in his chair.

Chapter Five

As if some kind of marriage ceremony, a metaphysical one perhaps, had been performed the evening Stefan had taken her to von Eschenberg's for dinner, Kitty Hammersmith had, at Stefan's suggestion, given up her suite at the Hotel Monbijou and moved into his flat for the two weeks before they left Berlin.

If Stefan wondered why Kitty had so quickly fallen for him, had truncated her European tour and moved in with him, he never showed it. Kitty ascribed his lack of surprise to male vanity. It had been evident from the start, with the girl friend at the night club, that he had plenty of it. And yet Kitty really had no complaints on that score. If anything, some of the prideful panache she had found very attractive about him had dissolved into too much deference. He was obviously moving on to new territory, with a new kind of woman, and he wanted it to be a success.

If she loved Stefan, it was in a way altogether surprising for her. Because it was a cliché and silly-sounding, she had ignored it: but it had been at first sight. The first look both of them took at each other that night in New York had produced an electric jolt. And then the fact that the officer she was to meet and seduce in Berlin should turn out to be him, as she had suspected . . . No, it was not love she felt, really; it was a kind of shock. She was mesmerized by the coincidence of it all.

After her second, private meeting with von Eschenberg, Kitty had gone to a bookstore specializing in music and bought the scenario to Wagner's *Parsifal*. Stefan would not return from duty until after seven. She had curled up with the soft manila-bound booklet on the living-room sofa and kicked off her shoes. The German was of the kind which brought students to despairs of boredom. But she slogged through it, even appreciating the poetry in parts as well as the high-blown drama of it all. Yet, when she had finished, she had little idea of why von Eschenberg had insisted she read it.

Soon afterward Stefan unlocked the door of the flat and came into the hallway, calling her name. Instinctively—she wanted to wait for the right moment—she hid the booklet under one of the sofa cushions. He had not yet told her the nature of his mission.

"I'm in the living room resting my feet. Spent the day shopping and bought nothing." Stefan walked through the doorway of the modestly proportioned modern flat and stood still for a second, his face radiant, taking her in from head to toe as she lay sprawled on the couch. There was a trace of amazement in the pleasure written on his face.

There was no calculation, no smugness in that look, she thought; there was only wonder in it and then passion. She was sure he was in love with her.

She watched as the tall, handsome, uniformed young man walked across the room to her, almost a heroic character out of an operetta—except for the true nature of the uniform and what it stood for. He bent down and kissed her, then knelt and continued kissing her more deeply. She wrapped her arms around his neck and gave herself up to his primordial attempt to devour her. He pulled away for a moment to look at her, his smile radiant, and began undoing the buttons of her blouse. He sprawled more comfortably on one hand as she fingered his uniform jacket, opening it, then his shirt. His mouth grazed over her lips, then down her neck. With the ease of habit, he reached around and undid the clasp which freed her breasts from the brassiere. He continued his exploration, breathing in the warmth of her flesh, his lips nuzzling over the ripe mound of her breast until they reached the pink areola of her nipple.

She did not know whether it was in the German national character or simply a characteristic of Stefan, but there was something crude, even pornographic in the way he made love. It aroused her enormously. His teeth began teasing the nipple until he was well over her threshold of pain. And then he sat back and stripped off his uniform, getting to his feet to slip off his shoes, then his trousers, then his underwear and socks, until he stood towering over her, his penis extended out to her. She found herself feasting on the sight of him, as she never had any more modest American lover. She slipped out of her clothes, then she lay naked and open to him.

And when finally he entered her, it took her breath away; she was ready as she had never been for any man before Stefan. Both her hands grabbed hold of his firm, lean buttocks, all trace of puritanical reticence long gone. They plunged and struggled after their orgasm together until the first whimpers from Kitty's throat signaled she had found it; with a brutal grunt Stefan drove himself deep inside her and climaxed.

In the growing dusk of the room Stefan lay, as if curled up, on top of her, his mouth nestled against her neck. Neither felt the urge to move, to disturb the peace they felt. It was as if together like this they managed to escape out of time, out of place.

When the telephone began to ring, it seemed far off.

The housekeeper had left promptly at six. Stefan let it ring. He was far away. There was no one in the flat to answer it. Finally it stopped.

It was the renewed silence in the room which forced them back to the here and now. Kitty felt one arm falling asleep. She moved it ever so slightly, but Stefan sat up.

"I'm crushing you."

"Don't be silly, darling. Just needed a little stretch." As if to prove it, she reached her arms high over her head, then plopped them both back down on the sofa at her sides. Stefan laughed lightly.

"You're . . . you're like a goddess, Kitty. There's something so strong about you . . . an Amazon."

"Are you insinuating, Herr Blauer, that I only have one tit? Surely you've noticed I have two, even if you only seem to pay attention to one of them." He laughed in embarrassment, like a boy chastened for doing something unmanly.

"I'll do better next time," he began.

She put her finger to her lips. "You *do* do better— the best." Silence followed as they beamed with pleasure at one another.

Stefan bent down and kissed Kitty on the mouth. Then he got off the sofa and began gathering his clothes together, neatly draping them over his arm.

"By the way," she said suddenly as she watched him tidy up, "I went to visit Hans von Eschenberg today."

"Oh?" He looked at her, startled.

"Yes, and he told me to read the scenario for Wagner's *Parsifal*. He was very insistent."

Stefan was shaken, she could see that. She had taken a calculated risk; she wanted him to begin confiding the nature of the mission to her. Then he smiled: "Are you going to?"

"Do you think I should?" His pause, his evident confusion, sent a chill through her.

"Hans is very keen on opera . . ."

* * *

The inner sanctum as well as the SS barracks in their entirety struck Blauer as parody of the conventional military headquarters. The black uniforms, the rakish, lightning-bolt SS insignia, the silver death's heads and the shining black leather reminded him of a cabaret skit in a brothel-Rathskeller he had managed to get in to see with a bunch of school chums that summer in Berlin before he went off to West Point. And like the skit, the SS reminded him of a perverse, decadent sexual longing for power. It shook his faith in the Third Reich, rather than reinforcing a sense of strength and renewal.

Kriegshofer, in particular, disturbed him. But, understandably because of his previous involvement in the Phoenix Formula operation, it was to him that Blauer was to report. Blauer, standing at ease in the SS general's office, now listened attentively to Kriegshofer. Instinctively Blauer was on his guard.

"Personally, Captain Blauer, I find a return to the Montségur area pointless. It has been scoured and all relevant persons questioned by many of our agents already, including myself. But the Tibetan considers it a good point of departure for you, and, in these occult matters, who am I to disagree." A smile flashed across Kriegshofer's sharp features, then vanished. He eyed Blauer coldly. "Perhaps you will succeed, Blauer, where others have failed." And then, appraising Blauer with the cutting depth of a surgeon's knife, he added: "Indeed, perhaps you will."

He turned away from Stefan to pace the room. When he turned around to face Blauer again, his expression had changed totally. His face radiated camaraderie and confidence. "Captain Blauer, the future of the Reich is in your hands. And I am here to aid you in every way possible. I might add that the Führer

himself is following your mission with keen interest;
he has given it maximum priority.

"Now, for final details." He went to his desk and
picked up a wax-sealed packet and handed it to
Blauer. "I have taken the liberty of having an American passport made up for you and your wife."

Blauer betrayed his surprise and annoyance:
wouldn't it further complicate things to have to remember he and Kitty were married?

"There is a problem, Captain?"

"Sir, Miss Hammersmith has agreed to come along,
but I have not really involved her in the details
of . . ."

"My dear Captain, you may do so. In fact, you
should. I have seen to her clearance personally. Con-
fide in her. Her allegiances are sound."

Blauer felt relieved. Kriegshofer's assurance dis-
pelled any feeling of risk he had had. The SS General
was taking personal responsibility.

"Thank you, Herr General."

"Then, I leave you to your task, Captain. Inciden-
tally, there is a large sum of money along with the
passport. It will serve to loosen tongues. You already
have the bank drafts for your expenses?"

"Yes, Herr General."

"And you will leave?"

"Tomorrow morning, sir."

"Then, *Sieg heil,* Captain Blauer." The two men exchanged raised-arm salutes.

As he left the barracks, Blauer glanced at his watch.
He had called von Eschenberg that morning at the
Ministry of Culture and asked to see him at home at
six P.M. With typical irony Hans had said he would
try to break free of the office in time. Blauer had not
laughed as he usually would have. He had been
peeved at von Eschenberg for having given information, however cryptic, to Kitty about his mission.

Now that hardly seemed to matter. He could see old Hans with nothing more on his mind than a fond farewell. And Blauer would be able to be on time; he had a half-hour to spare.

He dismissed his official driver and car at the War Ministry, then hailed a taxi. This was personal business. If he was being watched, let them earn their salary.

The cab left him off in front of the count's Charlottenburg mansion. Blauer spotted the SS man watching the house and smiled to himself. He was pleased at his ability to sense a spy.

Old Fritzl showed him into the salon. The two men embraced.

"Well, my boy, when do you leave?" Von Eschenberg gestured Blauer toward a chair as he sat down himself. "Drink?"

"Scotch, please." Hans reached over to the tray Fritzl had left on the table beside his armchair and poured two drinks. "Thank you, sir." Blauer took a sip. "We're leaving tomorrow morning."

"Oh? So soon? Then this is our last chance."

Blauer laughed. "I don't plan on being gone forever."

A thoughtful look crossed Hans's face, then was gone. "Oh, I mean this is our last chance to talk before you go. I wish you'd come by earlier."

"I would have, but . . ."

"Yes?" Hans sensed Stefan's hesitation. "Out with it, Stefan. I'm not dense. Something has come between us. It's the mission, isn't it? What have they told you about me?" The count's voice was stern.

"Did my father in fact draw up a horoscope on me which showed I was chosen to find this thing?"

"Yes, Stefan. I believe he did."

"Then why haven't you ever told me?"

"Well, it hardly seemed relevant up until now. Gerd was quite interested in the occult, you know. It be-

came a passion for him while you were away. And
then he began working with them and . . ."

"You didn't approve of my father working with the
SS?"

"I've always made that plain, my boy. I don't trust
them. And they know it, I'm afraid. That's why
they've got a man out there spying on me."

Blauer smiled and nodded. Yes, Hans had always
been frank about that; he had helped form Blauer's
own prejudices on his return to Germany in '33.

"But I don't have to tell you. You do know that I'm
being sent out in search of the Grail, preposterous as
that may be, don't you? What else do you know about
all of this?" Blauer strained to keep a light tone in his
voice.

"Kitty told you about *Parsifal*, then?"

"Yes, she did. Hans, you really shouldn't have . . .
but it doesn't matter now. I'm going to tell her all I
know about the Phoenix operation tonight." Hans betrayed his surprise. "The SS has officially cleared her.
I'm to tell her everything now."

"Cleared her? Who has?"

"Oberstgruppenführer Kriegshofer himself. Now
what do you know about the Grail?"

Von Eschenberg took a sip of his drink. This news
disturbed him, but he would have to make inquiries
before he could say anything to Blauer. And there was
no time.

"A good deal less than our Tibetan friend, Mr.
Langsung."

"You know the man?" Now Blauer was caught off-
guard.

"Yes, I do, Stefan. He was a friend of your father's.
And . . ." He tapped his fingers in a quick drumroll
rhythm on the arm of his chair. "And I think you
must trust in him. We must, both of us. There's no
one else."

* * *

The train to Paris left from the Potsdamer Bahnhof. From Paris they would catch a train at the Gare de Lyon, after a short stopover to make the necessary financial arrangements at a convenient French bank. There was no more direct route. France was totally centralized on Paris. Reaching Montségur would take another day and a half.

Briefly Stefan—now Steven—had explained to Kitty that they were in search of the Grail. "Like young Parsifal?" And she had laughed. He had decided not to dwell on it. There would be time later, and it was better that she ask the questions.

He had shown her their American passport. In it they were husband and wife—which amused her—but it seemed impeccable. Now as they boarded the train, Kitty wondered whether French customs would find it so. They now spoke only English together, and they looked and felt like honeymooners.

The morning train left punctually. From their private first-class compartment, wood-paneled, polished and overstuffed, they watched the verdant countryside pass by, began counting cows, then gave up in gales of laughter because they had both lost count.

"Germany is like Vermont, I suppose," said Kitty. Steven looked puzzled. "Everybody knows there are more cows in Vermont than people. You'll have to do better than that or no one will believe you're American."

"Then I'll just have to have you by my side at all times to get me out of situations where cows are involved." She began to laugh, then seemed to think better of it.

"I suppose that's why you have me along—to get you out of scrapes like that."

"That's the official reason."

Kitty wanted to push on further, but she thought better of it. "And the unofficial one?"

"Because I'd go crazy without you." They had been

sitting face to face by the window. Now he bent forward and kissed her on the mouth. His talk was extravagant, but Kitty believed him.

At lunch in the dining car, Kitty was surprised to find that the food was French.

"But isn't this a German train?"

"Yes, of course. But the restaurant belongs to the Compagnie des Wagons-lits and —"

"Shouldn't a good Nazi protest?" A portly man eating his soup across the aisle looked up suddenly.

"Well, you'd think they would, wouldn't you," replied Steven, playing the American to counter Kitty's slip. "They insist on everything else being all-German." The man raised an eyebrow, making it plain that he understood English and did not approve.

Kitty looked at Steven, then at the man as she said: "Well, dear, you know we always go on about things being all-American, like football players." The portly man nodded and went back to his soup. Steven untensed.

They ordered from the menu, printed in French and German only, with the help of the waiter and at times pretended not to understand.

"Guinea fowl, dear lady, if I may be of service," spoke up the portly man on the other side of the aisle.

"Oh, thank you, sir. My French is so poor, and neither my husband nor I know German at all."

"Such a pity, dear lady. One can hardly expect to understand and enjoy our Germany without speaking the language."

"Sure, language is important," interrupted Steven, as colloquially American as he could muster, "but you people over here in Europe speak so many of them. Can't take time out to learn three or four."

It was obvious that the portly man was not particularly interested in addressing Steven, but now he was obliged to. Reluctantly he turned his eyes away from Kitty to face him.

"Quite so, young man. But perhaps someday one will only need know German in Europe to get along."

"That hardly seems likely," broke in Kitty. The portly man bowed from the waist.

"As you wish, dear lady. But do not count on it." And he returned to his soup. He didn't say a word to them until he had finished all four courses of his lunch and gotten up from the table. Then he simply wished them a pleasant journey and was gone.

"What was that all about?" whispered Kitty.

"Pretty much nothing, I'd say. Just another decent German patriot. Don't Americans defend their country anymore?"

"Of course they do, silly. But they don't imply that the whole world will soon be speaking English."

"You mean American."

"Don't get cute with me. Just how many other good Germans are banking on world conquest beside that fat one?"

"Very few, Kitty. Really . . . You weren't in Germany before Adolf Hitler came to power. You have no idea of the misery, the national humiliation."

"No, I guess I don't. I just don't like talk about war, that's all." She backed off deliberately. Steven smiled at her tact.

"And neither do I. But Germany must be strong. She must take her rightful place among the nations." And what was that "rightful place," he thought to himself. He remembered Sebottendorf's words, then Kriegshofer's. Fortunately Sebottendorf and men like him had the ear of Germany's Reichsführers. The country was being wisely led.

Kitty decided to let the subject drop. They made their way back to their compartment in silence, Steven draping his arm across her shoulders. He ushered Kitty inside graciously, then drew the curtains on the corridor and locked the door. They would spend most of the afternoon making love.

* * *

The woman had been staring at them all through dinner or, more precisely, at Steven. Now she came up to them as they sat in the lounge sipping after-dinner cognac.

The train was swaying less now. They were slowing down. In an hour they would be at the French border, and the train would come to a halt. Blauer was positive that his American passport was beyond reproach. Still, it had never been tested. And he was nervous.

A throaty, hoarse-edged woman's voice broke his train of thought. "My name is Olga Bartok. May I sit down with you for a moment?" Turning to Steven, she added: "There is something I must tell you, sir."

Blauer found himself staring into the woman's eyes. They were a shade of green usually found in a cat's eyes and not those of an elegantly dressed woman most probably in her late fifties. There was something too girlish and compelling about them. Blauer turned to avoid them, a smile on his lips, and looked at Kitty. Blauer expected to find surprise, amusement or perhaps (he hoped) jealousy. Instead Kitty was watching the woman with a fascination bordering on admiration.

"Please do sit with us," said Kitty. The woman sat down. Kitty smiled across at Steven. He could have strangled her. Didn't she realize that these random contacts unnerved him, opened him up to the possibility of detection?

"Are you German, sir?"

Blauer snapped his attention back to Olga Bartok's question. The shock of it clouded, paralyzed, his mind for a split second.

"Funny you should say that. I'm an Amercian, but I am of German descent. Name's Blauer, Steven Blauer, and this is my wife Kitty." Olga Bartok smiled and held out her hand. Blauer shook it and then Kitty did.

"Americans are always something else, aren't they?

Of course," she added hastily as if fearing she had given offense, "so are many Hungarians like myself. There's a solid strain of Esterhazy in my veins, and of course that's very Austrian."

"I bet you have a title," Kitty interrupted enthusiastically. Blauer almost laughed, then realized that Kitty's silly American hunger for titles only further enhanced their American status.

Olga smiled and turned to Kitty with the benign smile of an adult toward a precocious child.

"Yes, Countess. But the Anschluss has made that a pointless matter I'm afraid, my dear."

"The what?"

"Austria is now just another province of the Reich. You are aware of that, certainly." Olga Bartok was obviously trying to check her exasperation.

Blauer interrupted. "We're not too in touch with what's going on in Europe back home, Mrs. Bartok . . . Countess."

"As you wish, young man." She turned back to Steven with evident pleasure, a seductive smile playing around her eyes. Olga Bartok was still beautiful enough—her almost naturally honey-colored hair done in an elaborate composition of braids and waves—that her coquetry did not appear totally absurd.

"But you are sure to be made aware of European events . . . and very soon," she added. Her expression had changed totally. "The growing strength of Germany is not a European affair only. This you will soon see. In Germany today there is a great struggle." She lowered her voice. "It is nothing less than the war between good and evil. It is like nothing else in human memory. It is the struggle between heaven and hell." Steven had to keep himself in check to avoid smiling at her melodrama. "And I fear the outcome. I fear deeply for the good. The good is very weak in Germany, Mr. Blauer. Very weak."

Steven glanced at Kitty. She was entranced. Olga Bartok had made his pleasure-loving rich girl deadly serious. The woman was obviously either a Gypsy or a Jew—if she ever did have a title, she could only have been stripped of it for those reasons. Her doomsday mouthings were absurd. The Führer would never start a war.

And then Steven remembered Kriegshofer.

"Shouldn't we all be getting back to our compartments? The French border is coming up soon, isn't it?" he said.

Olga Bartok frowned at Blauer. "We have plenty of time. Almost half an hour, Mr. Blauer. May I see your palm?"

"Oh, I think that's a little silly . . ." Blauer turned to Kitty for help. For some reason he did not want Olga Bartok reading his palm.

"Oh, go on, Steven. I think it's fascinating."

Resigned to the inevitable, Blauer extended his palm. Olga Bartok took hold of it immediately, palpating it, holding it up to the small fringed lamp to see the lines more clearly.

"I am not surprised, Mr. Blauer. It is what I thought. The Mystic Cross—a crucial destiny." She paused to take a small lorgnette out of her bead-studded evening bag. "May I examine more closely?" She put the glasses before her eyes and again held the palm up to the light. Abruptly, she let his palm go and put the lorgnette back in her bag.

"Are you familiar with the Holy Grail, Mr. Blauer?" A knowing smile played across her face. She sat back in her armchair. Blauer, stunned, held himself firmly in check.

"That's the Knights of the Round Table or something, isn't it?"

Kitty was looking at him curiously.

Olga Bartok ignored his reply. "You are a remarkable young man, Mr. Blauer." She rose to her feet. "May I wish both of you a good journey." She turned to smile at Kitty, then left the lounge.

The train's whistle sounded.

"That must be the French border, Steven. We'd better get back." Kitty stood up. "Wasn't she incredible?"

Blauer shrugged his shoulders and followed her quietly back to their compartment. But she had disturbed him deeply. How could she have known? Was his mission already compromised?

The train seemed to wait at the frontier interminably. Steven heard footsteps going up and down the corridor outside, but there was no knock, no passport check as yet. He grew increasingly nervous as time elapsed and there were more footsteps.

Kitty looked at him sympathetically. "You don't think there'll be any problem, do you, Steven?"

"Certainly not," he snapped.

Kitty chose not to press the point. She did not want to add to Steven's jitters.

Suddenly they both heard cries of protest in the corridor not far from their compartment. Steven jumped to his feet and slid the door open violently. A well-dressed man was being hustled down the corridor away from them between two brown-uniformed customs men.

"What is it, Steven?" Kitty stood up but could not see out the door. Blauer was blocking it. He stepped back into their compartment and slid the door shut again.

"I'd say someone's papers were not in order." He sat back down again and tried to compose himself. Kitty remained standing. For a second she seemed in a state of shock. He looked at her questioningly but she shook her head and sat back down.

"The man's cries—they were horrible. Like some animal being led to slaughter." She shuddered visibly.

"Come now, Kitty. Don't be theatrical. He's probably just some—"

"Some what, Steven?"

"Oh, who knows."

They were interrupted by a knock on the door.

"Vos passeports, s'il vous plaît, messieurs dames." The door slid open; a navy blue—uniformed French customs official half-entered their compartment. Behind him stood two brown-uniformed men wearing the insignias of the Reich.

"Passport, dear," Blauer said nonchalantly to Kitty. Steven slipped it out of his inside breast pocket and handed it to the Frenchman.

"Américains?" He did not look at either of them. He flipped through the husband-and-wife passport. He looked down at them for a second, then stamped it and handed it back to Steven. *"Voilà, monsieur."*

Blauer reached up for it.

"Say, do you speak English? What was all that commotion?"

"Very little, monsieur," he replied haltingly. *"Le désordre, monsieur."*

Kitty looked at Steven with surprise. She wasn't aware that he spoke French.

"Un juif, monsieur. Depuis leur 'Kristalnacht' . . ." The French customs man shrugged a shoulder back toward the two German officials standing behind him. *"Depuis ça, ces juifs courrent vers la France à bâtons rompus. C'est la pagaille. Comment voulez-vous qu'on laisse entrer comme ça! De toute façon, un juif c'est comme une punaise . . . faut s'en débarrasser, quoi. Bon voyage, messieurs dames."* The French customs official slid the door of their compartment shut.

"I didn't know you spoke French."

"You don't know everything about me, my dear." There was elation in Blauer's voice: the passport was sound.

"What did he have to say?"

"Oh, some Jew . . ." His voice trailed off. He was too flushed with this first successful passage to think of anything else.

"What about him? Steven!"

He cocked his head up at her. "About the Jew? Oh, he said something about lots of them trying to get into France ever since Kristalnacht. Then he said like ticks, you just had to get rid of them."

"Kristalnacht." Kitty said the word with no inflection. It was not a question. Briefly Blauer was surprised that she knew about the recent anti-Jewish riots in Germany, then he forgot about it.

Chapter Six

The Pog or peak of Montségur erupted out of the lush green of the mountains of the Languedoc like bone out of flesh. And on the topmost crag stood the ruins of the castle of Monsalvat, where the Albigensian heretics, locally called the Cathars, had stood their last ground.

The climb up to it from the village of Montségur was exhausting. Blauer and Kitty had had to stop to rest several times. It seemed impossible that an army had once stormed and conquered this redoubt. There was something unnerving to Blauer about the whole setting at the site of the massacre, something nightmarish. Even in the warm, bright June sun of southern France, the rock seemed icy cold, the stones of the ruined fortress corpselike.

But to Kitty it was all lush, beautiful countryside and bright blue skies. She found the climb exhilarating, and at times, her arm tucked in his, her stride almost pulled Steven forward.

"The view is just breathtaking. Better than Vermont and all her cows to boot!" she said.

They stood on the ramparts of the castle looking across the sharp fall of the valley miles below to the

other peaks which joined up with the Pyrenees. He
had to agree with her. It was spectacular.

"But don't you find the whole place gloomy? To me
there is something mournful about these mountains,
these stones." As they stood arm in arm, Kitty turned
to look at him. His expression was oddly troubled.

"Oh, you're such a silly romantic. At Vassar they always said that the heart of German romanticism was
black and funereal. And right they were. But that was
the nineteenth century."

"They should have told you that German romanticism did not end with the year 1900. We fought a
world war for it."

"Do you think you'll fight another one?" Her point-
blank question came as a total surprise.

"All I can say, Kitty, is that I hope not. Really I do.
Even though I'm a military man. The next war, if it
should come, would be worse than anything in living
memory. But, fortunately, the Führer does not want
war."

"Oh, I see." Her previously gay expression was gone.
Briefly she remembered Olga Bartok. And she remembered Helen's murder.

He gave her a short squeeze. She turned and smiled
at him, but she looked thoughtful. "What exactly are
you looking for here, Steven? Not some mythical
grail."

He took a deep breath. He had been expecting this.
In fact he had wondered that she had waited this long.

"This castle is the site of the last place on earth
where it was supposedly located."

"So what? It's all a legend."

"I would agree with you wholeheartedly, but—"

"You don't mean to tell me that you've been sent
out disguised as an American to look for some mytho-
logical spiritual object? That's what the Holy Grail is.
I don't believe it. Germany must be in the hands of

lunatics." She caught herself, but not quite soon enough.

Blauer flushed. He was somewhere between anger and embarrassment.

"It's the damned SS."

"Oh, you're all a pack of overgrown boy scouts."

"I wish you were right, Kitty. It would make things that much simpler." He thought for a moment. This was as good a time as any to begin explaining the mission. "Unfortunately, the Grail not only seems to be real—remember that Bartok woman? Don't you realize she must be after it? Look, it's real and it's a weapon. Not just a psychological one, Aryan legitimacy and all that, but a weapon of war, a formula for destruction. If I don't find it, someone else will. You can be sure of that. Can't you tell, the way they look at us around here?"

She nodded. Anyone would have noticed the quizzical looks, the smiles, the stares. "So how do you plan on going about getting it?"

Blauer frowned. That was just the problem. And then suddenly he began to laugh.

"I don't think that's so funny a question." Kitty did not like being laughed at.

"Not at all, Kitty. Not at all. I just realized something. You know why I was chosen? I was chosen because for some bizarre reason my father did a horoscope on me which pointed me out as the finder of the Grail. And they believe it."

"That's a lot of nonsense," she snorted.

"But don't you see, Kitty? They couldn't find it themselves, and this is supposed to be my special trump. Sometimes the wisest military tactic is to wait."

"Whatever does that mean?"

"That I'll just sit and wait. I've a hunch the Grail will sail right into my hands. Or at least solid word of it." He was not a particularly patient man, but it was

suddenly crystal clear that this was his set of options.
If there was any reason on earth for him to be there,
to succeed in the Phoenix mission where Kriegshofer
had failed, then he must rely on his father's predic-
tion. Seeing it that way in his mind, he suddenly felt
very calm. His father was touching his life from the
grave. It could only be for the good.

The small *auberge* they had put up at was also the
local café. When they tramped back, dragging their
feet with exhaustion, they were met with the sounds of
loud laughter and high-spirited French chatter.

After poking around the ruins some more and finding nothing except a gloominess which finally had
swallowed up both of them, the sound of human
voices now was grating, unbearable. Quietly they went
up to their rooms and laid down on the bed to rest
and relax before dinner. As they began to make love,
both of them fell dead asleep.

Blauer awoke in the dark. His watch read ten
o'clock. He shook Kitty awake.

"Darling, we've got to get downstairs fast and pray
that they still have something to eat. It's after ten."
She blinked and woke up. She coughed nervously.

"Steven, I just . . . well, I just was having this awful
dream and . . ."

"Better get dressed, Kitty. The dream can wait until
dinner, if we can get any." Blauer's radium-dial watch
glowed in the dark. He switched on the bedside light.
They got dressed hurriedly and went downstairs.

"Voilà le couple charmant d'Amérique!" The innkeeper stepped out from behind the desk. Blauer figured he was drunk or close to it. His heavy-set body
seemed to sway toward them; his jowled face was red.
"And I know, like so many of our visitors, you have
overslept and now you are hungry. Well, you have the
good fortune to have stopped at an *auberge amical*. I

am understanding. And the kitchen is still serving."
He finished by giving Blauer an obscene wink.

The innkeeper was disgusting. It was all Steven
could do to hide his anger and contempt. The man
might prove useful, however; he might know something about the whereabouts of the Grail or know
someone who did.

Steven returned his wink.

"My wife's a heavy sleeper," replied Blauer with a
convincing leer.

The innkeeper laughed gutturally. He motioned
them toward the dining room.

In one corner of the room was the bar, where a few
locals still stood drinking. The dining room was simply one end of the low-beamed café. The innkeeper
showed them to a small table furthest from the bar.
He stood over them as they sat down.

"Let me offer you an apéritif. Marcel, *deux pastis*,"
he called to the bartender without waiting for an ac-
ceptance or rejection of his offer. "What brings two
young Americans to this part of France? The honeymoon? But why our little village of Montségur, *hein?*
Marcel, you sleeping or what!"

"Coming, Monsieur Berteil," replied the harried bartender. He rushed to the table with two tall tumblers,
each with a finger of yellow liquor, and a small pitcher
of water and a small bowl of ice. The innkeeper put
ice in their drinks, then added some water. Instantly
their drinks became a milky color.

"You have tasted our pastis? Try it. Go on."

Kitty and Steven took a sip of the licorice-flavored
drink. They had both tasted pastis before, but for the
innkeeper as American tourists they pretended surprise,
then pleasure.

"Delicious," Kitty announced.

"I like it. What's it called again?" asked Steven,
looking up at Berteil.

"Pastis," he beamed. "Place yourselves in my hands.

I shall order dinner for you." He turned away from them abruptly and went off in the direction of the kitchen.

Kitty laughed quietly. "Quite a character, isn't he? Are you going to tell him what we're doing in Montsé-gur? He seems quite interested."

The "we" did not go by Steven unnoticed. He appreciated it.

"Perhaps." But Blauer decided he would stick to his decision. He would let fate act. Actually, he didn't know what else he could do.

Berteil returned to their table with a platter of hard sausage, bread and butter.

"Eat up now, my lovebirds. You like chicken? We have a beautiful *poulet basquaise*. But first the *saucis-son.* It is from the village." He put his fingers to his lips and kissed them, a parody of the gourmand. Blauer began to distrust him. He wondered whether Berteil would repeat his inquiry into their purpose for being in Montségur. He did not have to wait long.

"So, you have not told me. Why have you chosen our lovely town for your honeymoon, monsieur?"

"Well . . ." Steven began. "My wife and I are interested in, you might say, history. Especially the history around here."

"You know about the Cathars? Of course you do. So does everyone who comes here from the outside." Berteil's smug knowledge made Steven more uneasy. "And you are looking for something specific?" But Berteil was not really asking them a question; he was stating a fact he seemed to know as well as his own name.

"We belong to a society back in the States . . ." began Kitty.

"I know. I know." Berteil then began laughing. "All of you tourists belong to these societies, *hein*? You are not really German by any chance, are you?"

Blauer thought his heart had frozen in his chest: Berteil was toying with them.

"Why? You know we're Americans. You saw our passport when we checked in." Blauer tried to sound surprised, puzzled.

"*Le passeport?* One can buy and sell passports these days, monsieur. And there have been lots of Germans snooping about the Pog. They all belong to societies, too. What can I say? Germans take particular interest in our *petit* Montségur. They seem to be searching for something. Or some of them do," he added.

Steven played dumb. "What are they looking for?"

"I think you know perfectly well, monsieur. *Bon appétit.*" He turned and left the dining room.

"What the hell is going on here?" Kitty spoke in a hoarse whisper, but remained outwardly composed. They were always being eyed by someone in the room. She put her hand on Steven's and smiled. Steven leaned forward, and they kissed.

"Maybe he's just suspicious by nature. Or maybe he was Kriegshofer's contact. The SS already scoured this place."

"Then why in hell did they send you here?"

"Because they didn't find it. Obviously," he added, grinning.

"Oh, this is such nonsense. Of course they didn't find it. It doesn't exist."

"Well, I have a hunch our friend Berteil thinks it does."

Their conversation ended when the main course was served. It was delicious. The chicken in its sauce of peppers, tomatoes and onions on a bed of rice was devoured with great gulps of local red wine. Berteil, after serving them, had said no more, and disappeared into another corner of the *auberge,* leaving them alone in their candlelit corner of the rough-hewn room. The long shadows cast across the stone walls and up onto the beams were a constant reminder to Blauer of his confrontation with the SS in the dungeon hall at Vogelsang.

All at once he wished he could forget everything and just be alone with Kitty in this corner of a country inn late at night. But he could not.

At the bar two local peasants still stood drinking. It was approaching midnight. One of them was loud and obviously drunk. The other spoke more softly, teasing his friend into great belches of laughter while he kept an eye on the romantic foreign couple on the far side of the room.

After downing a large glass of local wine, the more sober of the two Frenchmen stood and crossed the room to stand at Steven's side.

"*Excusez-moi, monsieur.* I am Vaujean. You are German, *non*? *Deutsch*?"

Blauer turned to the man slowly. He had heard him approaching. Before Steven could reply, the man had pulled up a chair. From the bar came a cry of disgust from Cailleron, but the man sat down.

"No, we're Americans," Blauer replied slowly. He took in the wiry, dark-haired peasant rapidly. There was a glint, a rapid movement of his eyes, which betrayed the fact that he was coolly appraising Blauer as well.

"Don't get me wrong, monsieur. I have nothing against Germans. I did not fight in the last war. Germans never came here then. So . . ." he shrugged his shoulders and grinned. "But they do now. They are looking for something up on the Pog. They are looking, but they do not find." He grinned again.

"So it seems. Monsieur Berteil told us as much." Blauer was wary of this so-called peasant, but it was obvious that he could learn something from him.

"I know what they are looking for." The man spoke emphatically, but in a low whisper. He looked into Blauer's eyes with triumph.

"Oh?"

"Yes."

Neither man said a word. Blauer became edgy. He wanted the man to go on, but he seemed to have no intention of doing so.

"So what is it?" asked Blauer finally.

"Oh, some say they look for the treasure of the Cathars. But," he grinned and shrugged his shoulders once again, "there is no treasure, monsieur."

"No?" Blauer punctuated his reply with a sip of his cognac. Kitty watched the two men with fascination; they were ignoring her completely.

"Non, monsieur. But they are not looking for treasures, these *Bosches.* Not gold. Not jewels. *Non, monsieur."* Silence followed. It did not take Blauer long to realize what the man was leading up to: money. The men at Vogelsang had foreseen that; Blauer had left Germany quite rich.

"Interesting, monsieur," began Steven. "I belong to a society in America that might be very interested. We would pay for the artifact, of course."

"Of course, monsieur," replied the man laconically. He was studying Blauer carefully. Steven grew impatient. "You are from America?"

"We're from New York," interjected Kitty. The man turned to her as if surprised to see her at the table.

"Yes, madame. You are from New York," he stated flatly.

"What is this thing they are looking for?" Blauer finally asked outright. The man turned back toward him and smiled.

"The Holy Grail, monsieur. Imagine grown men looking for such a thing." He tapped the side of his skull, then got up slowly. "Sleep well, *messieurs dames."* He turned back toward the bar. "Cailleron, you coming or not?" They met in the middle of the room. Cailleron swung his arm around Vaujean's neck and, with loud good-byes, they staggered out of the *auberge*.

The bartender Marcel slipped out from behind the bar and left the room.

"*Schweinkopf!*" hissed Blauer under his breath. "He was just ready to—"

"I'd watch that," replied Kitty firmly.

Kitty lay fast asleep in the big bedroom. The room was pitch black except for a narrow ray of moonlight which crept in through a crack in the curtains. From the blinds shut on the outside of the window, the shaft of light was broken up. Blauer stared at it sleeplessly, imagining it was a ladder.

Vaujean had known everything Blauer was trying to find out. But he had not believed Blauer was American and he had not told him what he knew. Obviously he did not want the Grail to fall into German hands. It had to be as powerful an instrument as Sebottendorf claimed.

Suddenly Blauer wished he could extricate himself from the whole assignment. The Grail was fast losing its mystical trappings in his mind. Vaujean had been afraid. The Grail as the Phoenix Formula meant world mastery through blackmail or its actual use. Men would kill to have that power in their hands. Kill Vaujean. Kill him.

And then he remembered von Eschenberg. For the man's life and safety, he would have to keep on. But also for Germany's sake. With the Phoenix Formula in his hands, it would be safe from Kriegshofer and his kind. Suddenly the implications of his thoughts struck him: treason.

Treason, if he kept the Grail for himself.

His train of thought was broken by a tapping sound. It was almost inaudible. Then there was one loud rap on the door. Blauer, by instinct and training, had put a small military pistol in the drawer of the night table. He now slipped the drawer open and went to the door with the gun in his hand.

The floorboards creaked as Blauer reached for the doorknob.

"It's me. *C'est Berteil.*"

Blauer pulled open the door. The fat innkeeper stood blinking back at him, holding up a small kerosene lamp. "I have finally found out what you need to know. The woman, she is sleeping? Come out here quickly. Shut the door."

In his dressing gown Blauer stepped out into the hallway behind a fully clothed Berteil. He slipped the gun into his pocket. The innkeeper led him down to a room with the door half-open, light streaming out into the dark corridor. "Come in here. Quickly." Berteil's hoarse whisper was urgent, commanding. Blauer obeyed.

The brightly lit room was obviously Berteil's. It was neatly kept, the bed still unslept in and similar in furnishings to Blauer's own. Steven blinked his eyes to get used to the light. "Sit down please," said Berteil, motioning to an armchair.

Blauer complied. Berteil began pacing the room in silence. Blauer couldn't help but stare at him in amazement; Berteil was a totally different person.

"I couldn't tell Kriegshofer before," he began nervously, then turned abruptly to face Steven. "I didn't know. But now I do. Kriegshofer telegraphed that you were coming, Hauptmann Blauer. You can be frank with me. Did they send you here with plenty of money? Of course, my sympathies are with Fascism, *bien entendu.* My loyalty is not in question. That is not the point. But the risks, monsieur, my efforts, they must be reimbursed. I must get away from Montségur. I cannot wait for Kriegshofer. You will tell him. You can understand that?" His tone had become almost pleading. "You are not still playing the American with me, are you? Come, come! You are special, of course. They have never sent one like you." His eyes narrowed in his full, flushed cheeks. "You have powers, monsieur. There is no doubt. And you do not have the ways of the SS. You inspire confidence, you draw the Grail to you. Vaujean, for example."

"I don't know you, Berteil."

"You have been sent by Kriegshofer, *non*? You were not told of me? Well, perhaps your boss lost faith in me. But I knew nothing then. And he did want me to look for you. It is dangerous, monsieur. Vaujean has friends . . . look, monsieur, do not play with me. I know where it is. You have the money? Twenty thousand, monsieur. I keep my price."

"Where is it?" Blauer now smiled calmly. He slipped his hand idly into his pocket and felt the cold metal of the gun. He had not understood the references to Vaujean. But he had to Kriegshofer. There was something about Berteil that made him utterly contemptible. He was Kriegshofer's spy on him, and he was a traitor to his own country.

"It is not on the Pog, monsieur. It is no longer in Montségur," he went on, ignoring Blauer's question. "In 1905 it was found by a certain man, an Oriental, and he took it away. I have just learned this, monsieur. You must believe . . ." His voice became hoarse. "It is in a village in the Caucasus. You know that? In the east of Turkey. And, monsieur, I know the man in Istanbul who can take you there." His eyes now shone with pride; he was pausing to gloat.

For a split second Blauer thought he might pull the trigger. He stood up quickly. But he needed the name of the man in Istanbul.

"I'll go to my room, Berteil. The money is there." He left a nervous Berteil staring at his back. As he felt his way back down the pitch-black hallway to his room, he decided that he had no real choice but to pay Berteil and get the man's name. He believed Berteil.

Suddenly Blauer was convinced. If anyone should find this Grail, it was himself.

He returned to Berteil's room with twenty thousand francs stuffed in his dressing-gown pocket. He still carried the gun. He believed Berteil, but he did not trust him.

"Here, I have written it down. Turgut Salamyurek. Twenty-eight Yeniçeriler Cadessi. Istanbul."

Blauer handed Berteil the wad of French notes.

"Does he sympathize with the . . . with the Aryan cause?"

"He is a Turk, monsieur. His sympathies are for money. For sure." Berteil hurriedly leafed through the bills, then smiled back at Blauer. "Good luck, monsieur. *Bon voyage* and . . ." he paused, then saluted: *"Heil Hitler."*

"Heil Hitler," replied Blauer.

As Steven Blauer and Kitty Hammersmith got off the night train the next morning in Paris, the *Aurore du Languedoc* printed an odd news item under *Fait Divers*:

> "Double murder in village of Montségur. At six A.M. Thursday morning the body of a local farmer, Jacques Vaujean, was found . . . Twenty-four hours later, also in Montségur, the body of the local *aubergiste*, Gaston Berteil . . ."

A German with a thick, bullish neck left the newsstand at the train station at Clermont-Ferrand with the local newspaper of Languedoc under his arm. His face betrayed anger. There had been a settlement of accounts, as it were. He would be able to find out nothing at Montségur. His trip had been for nothing.

Outside the station the sky was low and gray. He pulled up the collar of his coat.

But Vebel now knew one thing: the Grail had been located. And most probably Stefan Blauer knew that location, as did the American spy with him.

"Fortunately Vebel is in Clermont-Ferrand waiting for orders, *mein Oberstgruppenführer*."

Häger's words did little to stop Kriegshofer's nervous pacing. Suddenly he reeled around, his rawboned features purple with anger. "Vebel should be in Montségur. *Schweinkopf!* You are all idiots. And where is Blauer? Don't you realize what has happened? Berteil murdered this Vaujean after getting the Grail's location out of him. Vaujean must not have been alone. His comrades avenged him. That's why Berteil was found with twenty thousand . . . *Scheize!*

"There is no time to lose. Where is Vebel exactly?"

Häger glanced at his watch; his hand was shaking. "He should now be back at the post office in Clermont, waiting for a return call."

"Good." Kriegshofer seemed to relax. "There is still a chance. He must get to Berteil's inn and get that information, then wire it to us through the regular code channels. Tell Vebel he has twenty-four hours maximum."

Häger snapped to attention: *"Sieg heil!"*

Kriegshofer returned the salute, and Häger left the office. Kriegshofer continued pacing his office alone.

So Blauer had the Grail's location. The large sum of money found with Berteil could have come from no one else but Blauer. The insane astrological timing had worked. Gerd Blauer's horoscope was correct. That poor fool Berteil.

Kriegshofer knew Berteil well. He had trusted him, but not far enough. He should have given him more information about his plans for Blauer.

But Berteil must have been desperate to get out of

Montségur once he had secured the information. He was not a rich man. He knew Blauer had the money he needed to get out of the country. And he, Kriegshofer, had even promised him that money himself when the time came.

Kriegshofer smiled wryly to himself. Desperation was not enough in Berteil's case. Nor was money. A good lesson: desperate moves must always be avoided. One must be calm; think clearly and rationally. And there was his own horoscope to consider.

He would keep his appointment with the Führer.

And he would tell him what would certainly be true in the coming hours: that he had located the Grail. Blauer would be denounced, he and his Zionist American spy girl friend. And it would be obvious to the Führer that he, Kriegshofer, had been right all along. Sebottendorf and, in turn, the Reichsführer, should never have taken the Phoenix operation out of his hands. The Führer would see no other course but to appoint a new Reichsführer and to eliminate Sebottendorf. He would leap at the chance, chuckled Kriegshofer to himself. He knew Hitler had always shared his own view: the formula in their hands, and then war!

So perhaps things had worked out for the best after all.

The intercom on his desk buzzed. Kriegshofer's adjutant secretary announced that his car was ready.

The Führer would be very pleased.

Kriegshofer stood gloating over the name and address on the sheet of paper in his hand.

"Vebel should be back in Berlin tonight, *mein Oberstgruppenführer.*" Häger's voice was exultant. The elation in the room was highly contagious.

Kriegshofer looked up suddenly from the information on the page and frowned comically at Häger.

"Mein Reichsführer, Häger," Kriegshofer corrected. "The Führer has just had that old fool and Sebottendorf arrested."

Häger saluted with fierce pride.

Kriegshofer gave a neat bow of the head and smiled at his ally. "Have you ever been to Istanbul, *mein Oberstgruppenführer?"*

At first Häger blinked with disbelief at his new rank. Then tears of joy and gratitude welled up in his eyes.

"Come, come, Häger. We must think of a suitable reward for Vebel when he arrives. He will report to me first?"

"Yes, of course, *mein Reichsführer."*

"Good. He will be exhausted from lack of sleep and the journey. We shall welcome him here, then send him off to a suite at the Kaiser-Wilhelm. Champagne. A woman. And then the poor man will suffer a sudden heart attack. A hero's death."

Häger turned pale. Kriegshofer patted him on the arm. "Vebel knows much too much, my dear Häger. We cannot run the risk." Kriegshofer shrugged his shoulders, smiling sadly. "Pity. Such a pity." And then suddenly he had a second thought. Kriegshofer laughed out loud: "I've just given Vebel a reprieve, Häger. We shall send Vebel after Blauer. Under the command of our very thorough friend Strang."

Bloody Strang, thought Häger. *"Jawohl, mein Reichsführer."*

Chapter Seven

The Marais, the quarter of Paris favored by the nobility of the seventeenth century as a convenient location for their town houses, now a rundown maze of foul-smelling streets, had become the Jewish ghetto. As the black Citroën taxicab took Kitty Hammersmith down the teeming thoroughfare of the rue St. Antoine to her appointment in a garret on the fetid rue des Rosiers, she felt exhilarated by the almost Oriental fervor of the street hawkers, the pushcarts loaded with vegetables or dry goods and the sheer numbers of people milling around it all. But like any ghetto, it was also depressing.

As she paid off the driver at the rue des Rosiers, depression triumphed. The narrow street stank of urine and garbage, as did the dark, dank staircase she trudged up to reach the garret rooms.

As she went up past a slit of a window which shed stale gray light on the staircase, she checked her watch. The train left from the Gare de Lyon in less than an hour. Blauer had left her cheerfully on the rue du Faubourg St. Honoré in front of Chez Worth, agreeing to meet her later at the train station. He hated shopping tours. In the meantime he would see to the luggage.

She knocked on the door.

"*Qui est-ce?*" An old woman opened the door without waiting for the answer. Wordlessly she stepped aside and let Kitty into the slope-ceilinged room. A man who could easily have been the old woman's husband sat at a small wooden table, painted white but scarred and chipped.

"Mademoiselle Hammersmith? Welcome. Welcome." He made to get up, then sat back in his chair. Kitty stepped forward.

"It seems we have located it," she began.

"Yes, I know. There were two murders in Montségur." His nasal voice kept a monotone.

The old woman moved behind Kitty to take a seat. None was offered to Kitty; there were no other seats.

She now found herself looking for a chair almost desperately; her knees were weak from the climb up the stairs and this news.

"Murders?" She looked around the room.

"Yes. A Monsieur Berteil and —"

"That was the innkeeper, the one who . . ."

"Precisely. But you have the information. You know where it is."

"Yes."

"And?"

"But I don't have the details. We are taking the Orient Express within the hour."

"Then we must hurry. You go all the way to Istanbul?"

"Yes."

"You will be contacted there, then."

"By whom?"

"He will make himself known to you . . . or she . . . It is of no consequence. But you must find out more, mademoiselle. Where it is."

"He hasn't told me. Only about Istanbul."

"But it is not *in* Istanbul?"

"No, I don't think so."

"Has he lost confidence in you? He does not suspect . . ."

"No. No, nothing like that. I'm sure of it."

"Then you must find out more." The old man stood up. "And now your train, mademoiselle. And . . . you will please thank our friends in New York." The man's thanks seemed perfunctory, almost ironic.

Kitty felt ashamed. "We are doing all we can."

"Yes," he sighed. "I am sure. But many will die. Many have already. Many more than we know even. But there is still Palestine. And for now the British are a help, but for how long?" He shook his head. *"Au revoir, mademoiselle. Et merci!"* This time as he spoke to her in French, she felt warmth and gratitude to her personally. Did he know that she was not a Jew? He must. She suddenly glanced at her wristwatch. She had a half-hour to make the train.

"Thank you. I'll do my best." They shook hands.

As she pushed her way through the crowds in the Gare de Lyon, she located the *quai* from which the Orient Express was to leave. Unbelievably the train seemed slowly to be moving out. As she rushed past the ticket check, the *contrôleur* shouted after her to see her ticket.

Kitty ignored him and ran. She had not been able to find a taxi immediately on the rue St. Antoine, and now she was in danger of missing the train.

Despite her near panic she realized coolly that Blauer was not waiting for her on the platform. He was still much the Wehrmacht officer. Duty came first.

She caught hold of the door handle of the first compartment she reached, swung it open and jumped in, pulling it shut behind her.

A little girl squealed with delight. Two nuns commiserated with her in French. The little girl's mother looked at Kitty coldly and slapped the child quiet.

Kitty had fallen into a seat. Now she stood up shakily, smiled politely at everyone, opened the door to the corridor and shut it firmly behind her. She stood up tall and took a deep breath. Fortunately she had her ticket in her purse. A conductor came toward her a bit menacingly. Not speaking much French, she simply handed him her ticket. It was for a deluxe first-class sleeping-car suite. He nodded to her respectfully and led her through the train to her compartment.

"Kitty, what happened to you? I was worried to death." Steven rushed toward her and hugged her in his arms. She pushed him away slightly.

"Well, obviously not worried enough to wait for me!"

"But we had agreed to meet—"

"Oh, forget it, darling. I'm here. I just couldn't get a taxi."

"And where are your packages?"

"I couldn't decide. I didn't buy anything after all." She slumped into a great red overstuffed armchair.

Blauer came over, bent down and kissed her. "Are you really angry with me?" Their lips were inches apart.

"No. No, you were right. You have no time to waste."

Steven suddenly straightened up. "You're right, of course." He saw Kitty now in a new light. She should be told of his decision. At that very moment her clearheaded reply had helped him make it: he, and he alone, would take possession of the Grail.

* * *

The Parisian sky was spectacularly and unusually cloudless for spring, the air freshened by a faintly floral breeze. The late-afternoon light was golden as it reflected off the gilt of the Opéra beyond the teeming rue du Faubourg St. Honoré below, and gradually disconcerted her enough so that she suddenly pushed both wings of the french doors shut at once and bolted them. Olga Bartok touched at a curl of honey-colored braid at the back of her head. She walked slowly across the bedroom of her small suite at the Hotel Meurice and sat down before the dressing-table mirror.

She glanced abruptly at her wristwatch and bit her lower lip: Romanenko would be downstairs ringing up in ten minutes and before her in less than fifteen. Despite the gesture toward enterprise which his small and very esoteric bookshop on the boulevard St. Germain represented, he was typical of the breed of White Russian not impoverished by the events of 1917 and even of many of those who were; he was punctual. Tea with a woman of rank took precedence over all. And in a generally indolent, studiedly carefree existence, punctuality, the virtue of princes, was easy.

Romanenko had been a natural choice to handle the Bartok funds placed in France. Indifference made him scrupulously honest. Her husband had been wise to choose him. But the man bored her. If it were not for the occult interests which they all shared, she would not have two words to say to him.

That was not the case with all adepts of the esoteric. Gerd Blauer had been quite the opposite (his son—a surprisingly moving sight for her—seemed just as fascinating in his own right, though evidently not an *ésotérique*). And von Eschenberg—she caught herself smiling in the mirror. The last of the *bons vivants*: witty, ironic, charming; she would like to have spent more time with him in Berlin. She regretted not having looked him up earlier. But events had . . .

It was hard to believe that only seven years ago she and her husband had been seated, not a care in the world, in a café on the Via Veneto, enjoying the parade of Romans, of Easter tourists to the Eternal City, of lovers heading toward the gardens of the Villa Borghese and of girls and boys wrapped up in the serious commerce of selling their bodies under the great pines along the garden's edge. She had found the male prostitutes particularly fascinating.

"Which one do you fancy, madame?" Gerd Blauer had been so impertinent she had laughed outright. Bartok, diligently trying to decipher *Il Messaggiero*, had looked up startled at this stranger's intrusion. He had not understood a thing. But the stranger spoke German, his wife seemed amused, and so he, too, began to smile. The newspaper seemed gratefully forgotten as Bartok sat back and let himself be amused by Blauer's satiric comments on the passersby.

"Touring in Rome, I take it." Bartok was a generous man, oblivious of the existence in the world of jealousy. And now he questioned Blauer with friendly enthusiasm.

"Not really, *mein Herr*. Studying, actually. Some curious things lay in the Vatican Library." He had no need to say another word. It was an opener for Bartok's favorite subject.

"They say the entire corpus of Black Magic, among other things."

"Why, yes . . ." Gerd Blauer suddenly frowned and looked away briefly. The air of banter vanished. When he faced them again, his eyes examined them curiously. "You are interested in that kind of thing?"

"Very." Then Bartok had turned to her. "And my wife Olga has some quite amazing natural gifts in that respect."

Blauer had touched his fingers to his forehead in a gesture of respect. "And remarkable green eyes . . ."

She had found herself blushing, quite unlike the girl she had been thirty years younger, when blushing would have been more appropriate. Her mother had impressed on her that for a woman to be taken seriously by men, a cool head was essential and must be basic to her nature. Olga had surpassed her mother in that virtue. Fortunately, she had thought at the time, such a peccadillo had come upon her in her forties. And then she had glanced at her husband, only to be disappointed at finding not a trace of jealousy. He was more constant than herself. She went on from that moment with a new respect for him.

"Green eyes," Blauer had gone on, unperturbed, "are often a sign of such gifts. I don't know why . . ." Blauer, on such an inconsequential point, had seemed to drift off into thought.

"I thought only clerics got to use the Vatican Library." Bartok had no intention of letting a man of similar interests to his own escape so easily.

"Pacelli," muttered Blauer as if it were an adequate reply.

"Pacelli? I don't understand, Mr. . . ."

"Blauer, *mein Herr*. Gerd Blauer."

Bartok had then taken time out to introduce himself and her.

"Well, Pacelli is Vatican Secretary of State now. Since '29, I believe. I knew him in Berlin vaguely. So did many other people, I'm afraid. But he remembered who I was when I sent a letter off to him."

"You're a fortunate man, Herr Blauer. I'd give anything to get in there and take a look around."

"The Catholic Church has always entertained a very perverse, perhaps even an all-consuming, interest in the black arts." She had found it odd that Blauer had laughed at that point.

"And in pornography, it would seem," Bartok had

countered, joining in the joke. And then Blauer had grown suddenly serious.

"That's why I'm let in."

"Because of pornography, Herr Blauer? Come, come!" Bartok had gone off in a peal of guffaws. She had ignored her husband's joke and pressed Blauer. She had felt he urgently wanted to impart something.

"Why are you let in, Herr Blauer?" She had succeeded in sounding only interested, not inquisitory.

"The NSDAP, to be exact." Blauer's revelation sobered Bartok immediately.

"You don't mean to tell us you are a Nazi Party member, Herr Blauer. You hardly look the sort."

"Don't I?" Blauer's reply had been more statement than question.

"Of course," went on Bartok, ignoring Blauer's remark, "I suppose the priests are in cahoots with the Fascists, Mussolini and his crowd. Have to be, don't they really? But why Hitler's people? Makes no sense."

"Really?" Blauer had laughed.

"You have quite a sardonic sense of humor, Herr Blauer," Olga had put in immediately.

He had turned to her admiringly. "As natural as your green eyes, Madame Bartok."

"Well, let's not talk about politics. It's a bore. What I'm interested in, Blauer, is what you've found in the Vatican."

"Then let's have dinner this evening, if you two are free."

"Splendid." Bartok had glanced at her to get her approval.

"I think that would be charming, Herr Blauer." Yes, after all, she had thought, there was something conspiratorial between Gerd Blauer and herself. But it was not sexual. Bartok had no need to be jealous, and jealous he was not.

At dinner she had found Blauer's conversation as

fascinating as her husband had. That evening for the first time she had learned of the Grail. At least of the Grail as something real, beyond myth and operatic nonsense.

How she wished now that she never had.

And the circle was closing in. Pacelli had just been made pope: Pius XII.

The bedside phone rang, breaking her train of thought. The desk announced Monsieur Romanenko. She asked to be switched over to room service and ordered tea.

"Comment allez-vous, chère madame?" He kissed her hand and looked at her with the earnestness of his question. "I know these past months have been very difficult for you, and I . . ." He continued on, moving into the sitting room with balletlike formality, taking his seat after she took hers, chatting on, but she hardly listened. His appearance struck her: he had aged. His once broad, thin shoulders were stooped. He had a small paunch. His once blond hair, combed back severely from a high, angular forehead, was an unflattering tone of gray. But as he continued, he was once again the same old snob, high-strung, *fin de race*.

Tea arrived. She poured. And then they went through financial matters. She was a bit better off than she had thought. And the bulk of cash was in Swiss francs.

Then she came to her little surprise. She was curious as to his reaction, his opinion.

"You know of von Eschenberg in Berlin, don't you, Pierre?"

"Von Eschenberg? Name sounds familiar. Title?"

"Count." She couldn't help smiling.

"Ah, yes. Yes. Yes. Friend of that Blauer fellow. Weren't they all worked up over the Grail? Fascinating, really. Seems the Germans are keen on finding it."

"Oh? How do you know that?"

"Well, my dear Olga, I've heard they've been all over Montségur like flies on honey cake. Those peculiar Nazis . . ." He chuckled, then realized that she did not find Nazis amusing. He cleared his throat abruptly, erasing his amusement. "Must be up to no good."

"I saw von Eschenberg in Berlin only a few days ago. He told me something most alarming, Pierre." She paused to refill his cup, offering a cucumber sandwich. "They have gotten Blauer's son to search for it."

Romanenko seemed puzzled.

"Why the alarm? They'll never . . ."

"But they will, Pierre. Von Eschenberg has assured me. The holy innocent. Furthermore, I had a chance to see the young man's palm."

Romanenko raised both eyebrows. "You're positive of this? Preposterous, really."

"I saw it, Pierre. It is only a matter of time."

"Damn foolish of that Blauer to connive with those Nazis."

Olga nodded her total agreement.

"But Gerd Blauer was an innocent in his own right."

"Well," he sighed, "I never had the pleasure of meeting the man . . ."

"Pierre, don't you realize the danger?"

He frowned. "I do indeed."

"It will not only bring them legitimacy, but von Eschenberg is positive that the Grail holds the key to atomic change. That man Einstein's energy quotient. The SS would seem to agree; they refer to it as their Phoenix Formula."

"Oh, that's all hypothesis, my dear Olga. Einstein's just a quirky old Jew."

"Nonsense. And he's not old. He's working in America right now. They take him quite seriously over there."

"Well, what do you expect, Olga? It's a young country. They have no sense of proportion."

"Pierre, you are going to make me lose my temper. It means a bomb, weaponry, hideous destruction! In a word: total power over the world."

Romanenko paled. "Really? I . . ." He began to tap the fingers of one hand in sequence on his knee.

"Something must be done. They must be stopped."

"Herr Hitler's not interested in a war, my dear. He's got quite enough to do in Germany."

"Don't be naïve, Pierre."

Her contempt was too much for him; his face reddened. "A far sight better than the Bolsheviks!"

"He's going to make a pact with them."

"Now you are the one talking nonsense, my dear Olga: It's preposterous what you say."

"Von Eschenberg swears it's so. I believe him, Pierre."

"How could things take such a turn . . ."

"There's a new force in the Third Reich. Haven't you gotten wind of it?"

"The devil I—"

"Precisely."

"What?" And then he thought a moment. "So what's to be done, Olga? You've come this far."

"I've thought of contacting the Zionists, the Jews. What do you think of that idea? They have money, spies, terrorists . . ."

"Oh, no, my dear. That's surely the wrong course, getting caught up with that lot. I don't approve, Olga."

"Well, Pierre, that's what I wanted to know. Your opinion." She got up.

He stood immediately. "You aren't going to get involved with them, are you, Olga? They're so disreputable."

"Well, Pierre, I'm rather disreputable in German circles these days." A look of alarm swept across his face. She laughed. "No, Pierre, don't worry. I won't see them. But you must help. You must think of something."

"I'll try, Olga. But, really, I don't think it's all that urgent. I've been a student of these things for many years longer than you have, and, frankly, I don't believe the Grail exists. It's a sham. Something like the Indians making up El Dorado to send the Spanish off packing to their deaths in deserts and jungles."

"Perhaps you're right. Perhaps von Eschenberg is an alarmist."

He patted her arm. "I'm sure of it, my dear Olga. Quite sure."

When he had gone, she returned to her bedroom and the window. It was no longer as bright and sunny. A few fleecy clouds studded the sky, blocking the sun from time to time.

And then she went to the telephone by the bed. She read off the number with the Marais "Turbigo" exchange on a piece of paper lodged under the phone. The hotel operator put her through.

The day was ending in one of those absurdly theatrical Parisian sunsets, where clouds are illumined gold and pink from beneath and the west is a prism of color. The black Citroën taxi was taking her as fast as possible down the rue St. Antoine, away from the dirty garret of the rue des Rosiers to the elegant parade of the boulevard des Capucines and a drink at the Café de la Paix.

Olga was annoyed. She expected that confiding in the Zionists, offering them her aid in the Grail matter, would give her a sense of accomplishment—of revenge, in a way—on the hoodlums in power in Austria, a feeling of peace after all these months. But it hadn't. She had found the little old man insistent, obsequiously

Jewish. Romanenko had been right. Dealing with the Zionists had been distasteful. But what choice did she have? She had even agreed to go to Istanbul.

The taxi stopped, held up by an *agent de police* intent on allowing another street of traffic to cross the intersection. Irritably she watched the men and women milling home from work, jumping on overcrowded autobuses, crowding sidewalks. There was an air of gaiety in the streets. It was a beautiful warm day. Summer was not far off. And then there would be the workers' month-long vacation in August, only recently won by the last government, the socialist *Front Populaire*. What fools, she thought, what arrogance to think that their life could go on with its little pleasures, its new leisure for all, while the rest of the world, or at least of Europe, suffered or waited in fear. They considered their army the best in the world: the Undefeatable, as it was always referred to. And the Ligne Maginot on the Rhine facing the Reich: impregnable. Fortress France. The fools!

At least the little old Jew in the rue des Rosiers was more sanguine.

"Yes, I agree, madame. The Grail is a truly dangerous weapon. War is not far off. And that is why in Istanbul you will meet our man Silver. British. A man who has proved his worth in Palestine. A member of the Irgun Zvai Leumi." He had gotten to his feet and now beamed with pride. "A Jew can be a fierce fighter."

"Against women and children and a pack of backward Arabs?" She had supposed the man Silver was a terrorist. She was right; the old man flushed with anger.

"It is not quite that simple, madame. There have been Arab atrocities against our settlers."

"Whatever *is* simple," she had sighed. And then she had reiterated her true interest: fate. She was one of the many hands of fate free to impede this menace.

She spoke to him of the future, of occult doctrine, and, as if to force him to see her point more clearly, she reminded him of the Kabbala and the ancient interest of Jews in the Occult. Some said that the Grail was actually the Hebrew Ark of the Covenant. If so, it was rightfully theirs. He had nodded, smiled and shrugged his shoulders. He was a man who dealt with realities: his people were being slaughtered. He believed in the power of the Grail because his enemy believed in it. Period.

And so she had agreed to help get the Grail.

The taxi had started up again, and already she could see the Louvre with its great mansards. At the Café de la Paix she was fortunate to get a table on the crowded terrace. She looked around after she placed her purse on the tabletop and removed her gloves. She brushed back the short veil on her hat. Its feather darted back and forth as she looked at her fellow customers. One young man particularly struck her fancy. He was extremely handsome—beautiful, really—she thought, with his wavy brown hair, perfectly aquiline profile and full lower lip. He felt her eyes on him and looked over at her and then smiled. She smiled back. He had given himself away in that smile. It was pure feline. She would have him. They would dine together that very evening. She was sure of it. At her invitation, of course, at her expense. That's the way she had come to like it.

The waiter stood before her, surprising her. She glanced up in the direction of his white jacket, but did not bother to look at his face.

"*Un Dubonnet, s'il vous plaît.*"

She glanced back in the direction of the young man. He caught her eye and smiled once again.

Kitty awoke the next morning before Steven. She crawled out of bed quietly and put on her silk robe, going into the sitting room to an armchair by the window.

The train was stopped in a small station she did not recognize. The night porter took care of passports and customs. A loudspeaker out on the platform squawked and sputtered unintelligible directions and schedules. She could not make out the language; they could have been anywhere.

She usually did not smoke in the morning, but now she lit a cigarette as she stared idly out the window.

The light of early morning often made her queasy. There seemed something nervous and harsh about it. Perhaps they were in the south of Switzerland or the north of Italy; the July sun promised to be merciless by noon. Now shabbily dressed railway workers trudged in gangs of four or five across the platform and out of the station to work on the tracks further up. They wore the same Depression caps men wore back in the States. In fact there was very little about them which would give an impression of foreignness.

She had never given it too much thought, but perhaps all workers did belong to the same family of man, a family very distinct from the middle classes or the rich. Perhaps one day they would recognize each other from country to country and unite. The message of Soviet Russia.

Her father had been one of those workers. Or so her mother had told her one evening when the two of them had eaten dinner alone together in the great Park Avenue apartment. It had been her seventeenth birthday. Kitty, her mother and her stepfather were to have had a quiet party together at home. The cook, Mazie, had made the most unctuous chocolate cake she had ever seen and then eaten. But her stepfather had been called back to his Wall Street firm. Kitty had pouted; she loved her stepfather—a generous man ten years older than her mother, fatherly from his pipe to his slippers and reading the evening paper in his favorite red-leather winged armchair in the library. But her mother had stopped her sulking with a terse reminder that money, the making of money, often took precedence over everything. Especially in those first harried, dark years of the Depression. And then her mother had talked about her real father.

Kitty had never seen him, and her mother had never talked about him before. But what had shaken Kitty even more was that her mother talked about money and about not having any. It had scared her. It was her real seventeenth birthday present, Kitty now thought to herself. Her first brush with the world of struggle, misery and hunger—all of which her mother had described firsthand from her days with Kitty's father.

She wondered now whether any of these trainmen were secretly poets or painters, a painter like her father who, to support the spoiled rich girl who had run off with him, had been forced to go to work in a factory from six in the morning until six at night, only to come home to a rooming house, stinking of leather hides, too tired to hold a brush, and the light gone anyway. There were some men—and when her mother had begun saying these words, an anger which Kitty had never seen in her before crept into her mother's voice—there were some men who did not have it in them, no matter how much they tried, to withstand the bludgeon of the factory. The spirit went out of them, and then even a winter cold could kill them.

A shiver came over Kitty now. She took a puff of her cigarette, then put it out. She did not like smoking before breakfast; her mouth tasted awful. The train lurched and then began slowly pulling out of the station. She watched through the window as her car slowly passed the gangs of men who stood gawking at the great train passing them.

So Berteil, the innkeeper, and another man had been killed already in this bit of Nazi insanity. When the old man on the rue des Rosiers had told her, she had felt fear for herself for the first time since traveling with Blauer.

And perhaps she had deliberately tried to miss the train. She could have gotten out of it all then and there, gone back to New York, done something else with her zeal for justice or whatever it was that possessed her to help in the struggle of another race for survival. But the fact was that she had not missed the train. Perhaps she had remembered Helen. And Blauer, whom she loved despite herself, slept peacefully only a few feet away in the next compartment.

It had been difficult sleeping, wondering whether he had had anything to do with those murders. Something told her now that if she couldn't take it, she had better get off the train at the next stop. It would be her last chance to extricate herself. But then she dismissed this feeling of hers. She was not a quitter; and besides, everything about her assignment thrilled her—even, she realized with surprise, the murders. She felt more awake, alive and exhilarated than ever before in her life.

"Up early, darling?" Steven yawned as he came into the sitting room.

Kitty jumped in her seat. "Oh, you startled me."

Blauer smiled back and shrugged his shoulders in apology. "Any idea where we are, Kitty?"

"Not the slightest," she said, standing up. "Shall I ring for coffee?"

"The train will be in Budapest tomorrow morning when we get up," said Steven. Dinner was over. He had taken to smoking thin Havana cigars and now bit off the tip of one and lit it as the waiter poured their brandy.

"What's Budapest?"

"A day and a half from Istanbul, among other things," he replied. She smiled at him. She liked the dryness of his mind. They were well suited. She set aside her romantic urge; Blauer seemed in a mood to talk. He had been so subdued for most of the trip that she had wondered whether he knew about the murders in Montségur. But if he did, he never let on.

"And then what?" She took a sip of her cognac, then set it down on the white linen tablecloth. The waiter arrived with the bill, which Blauer paid immediately. When the waiter had left, Blauer smiled at Kitty.

"And then, darling, the Caucasus." He enjoyed her look of surprise, chuckling, then taking a puff off his cigarillo.

"I don't think I even know where that is," she began.

"Eastern Turkey, for our purposes. That's the part of the Caucasus Mountains where it is." He laughed outright now at her shocked expression.

"You know exactly where this thing is? It really exists?"

"Yes, I really believe it does." His tone had changed, had become thoughtful. Kitty shook her head in disbelief. "Well, you don't have to come along. In fact I have no intention of letting you. I've done a little research into the matter. The terrain is much too rough for a woman."

"Nonsense."

"I'm afraid not. You will stay in Istanbul and shop the Grand Bazaar to your heart's content."

"But I want to come along. I've gone hiking in mountains before, silly."

"Where? Vermont?" He was laughing at her.

"Yes, among other places," she replied defiantly.

"Did the natives carry rifles and have an acute taste for white female slaves, not to mention a fierce inhospitability where strangers are concerned?"

"Then they'll shoot you, and where will we be?"

"You'll be back in Istanbul eating Turkish delights and I'll be with my guide and quite alive, thank you."

"I didn't know you knew anyone in Istanbul."

"I don't yet. But I will. The day after tomorrow."

"And where did this guide person come from?" She took another sip of her cognac. Steven smiled and stood up slowly from the table, giving Kitty time to follow. "I won't get up until you tell me."

"Let's go into the lounge, Kitty darling. The cigar, you know . . ."

"I won't."

"Suit yourself." He turned and started out of the dining car. Kitty got up quickly, afraid to look around her, sure that everyone was watching their little contest of wills, and followed him out.

Blauer found a nice corner of the lounge and stood while Kitty sat down first.

"Where did this guide come from, Steven? You're not going to hold out on me now, are you?" She watched, somewhat surprised, as he considered what she said.

"No," he sighed, "I suppose not." He hesitated.

"So, where did—?"

"From Berteil." He seemed to ignore the fact that she had turned very pale. "He made a little visit at night while you were asleep. He told me everything. And I paid him what he asked for." Kitty trembled visibly. "You haven't caught a chill, have you?" He leaned forward.

He seemed to be showing real concern, she thought, as she only glanced at him, afraid to look him straight in the eye, afraid of what she might read there. "No. It's the brandy. I must have taken a gulp of it." She now felt back in control of herself.

"You don't mind if I sit and chat with you a bit, do you?" boomed a hearty voice. They looked up to find a stout, tall man looming over them, impeccably dressed in the best evening clothes Saville Row could sew together. He seemed the caricature of the proper Englishman, down to his spats. "I heard you speaking English and I can't bear to speak French or some other beastly foreign tongue. May I?"

Kitty sensed that Steven was on guard at once. Still he was gracious, stood up and introduced himself and Kitty. The Englishman shook Blauer's hand and bowed in Kitty's direction.

"The name's Reginald Cranston-Jones. Just Reggie, really." He pulled up an armchair and sat down as if they were all sipping after-dinner port in front of the fire at his country house. "You're American, aren't you?"

Blauer relaxed. "Yes, we are. My wife and I are on our honeymoon."

Reggie beamed at both of them. "So nice to see a pair of newlyweds. May I?" He signaled to the lounge steward.

"Yes, sir?"

"A bottle of Dom Perignon—1908, if you have it."

"Very good, sir. I think we do," he said with obvious pride, and went off to get it.

"Very good year, 1908," he said, turning to both of them.

"You really shouldn't," Kitty piped up. She didn't want it. Both she and Steven had had quite enough to drink already. She suspected suddenly that he meant to get them talking. A look from Blauer showed that he thought the same.

"But I insist. Besides, I love champagne, and since I'm traveling alone, and one can't very well drink a whole bottle oneself—now can one?—well, you are both doing me a great favor. By the way, going as far as Constantinople . . . or what do those Turks call it now, Istanbul?"

"Yes, we are," replied Blauer, tensing slightly.

"Never been there before, I suspect."

"Yes, you're right. You have?" retorted Blauer.

"Oh, yes. Actually I live there part of the time. Business reasons, I assure you."

"And you don't call it Istanbul?" said Kitty. Blauer smiled at her when Cranston-Jones turned to Kitty to answer.

"A bit of a reactionary, eh what? That's what you're thinking, Mrs. Blauer, I know. Well, perhaps. But I find that thinking of it as Constantinople somehow makes the city more palatable, more romantic, really. The reality is quite the reverse, I'm afraid."

"How do you mean?" she asked.

"Oh, that Atatürk got them to put on fedoras instead of fezes, and now they think they're European. Even taken up our alphabet. Well, to my mind it's all quite silly and, you know, unesthetic. That's it. Unesthetic. Turks in sheep's clothing, as it were, all dressed up like French *boulevardiers*. Dreadful. But I suppose finally I'm just betraying my age," he added, looking from Kitty to Steven.

"Well, we're looking forward to seeing some of the sights," said Steven, figuring it was as good a reply as any.

"Ah, here's our bottle," Reggie announced as the steward appeared with the Dom Perignon already firmly rooted in a silver ice bucket. A waiter followed with a tray, balancing three glasses. The steward poured. Reggie raised his glass. "To the sacrament of matrimony. May it see us through these trying years."

Puzzled slightly at the toast, Kitty and Steven drank up.

"What an odd toast, Mr. Cranston-Jones," said Kitty.

"Reggie, please."

"Reggie," she corrected. "And please: Kitty and Steven," she added, looking at Blauer.

"Thank you, my dear. Well, I should explain simply that my parents divorced when I was away at school—quite a scandal in those days, I might add—and, well, I myself have been ill fated within the bonds of that holy institution."

"I see," Kitty replied, then hesitated. "But you still believe in marriage?"

"I do indeed. Fervently. As I believe in all our Western institutions, sorry as their state may be."

Blauer smiled. "I must agree with you," said Steven. Kitty frowned almost imperceptibly, but Blauer caught it. They had had an unexpectedly virulent exchange of views in that regard just the previous night. She had been quite convincing, or he was actually wavering under the pressure of the Grail search, or perhaps he was too much in love with her for his own good. He wasn't sure. But he had been startled to find himself changing—and changed—in many ways.

He had realized with surprise that he did not trust his own country anymore. About anything. Had it been something Berteil had said that night? He couldn't put his finger on it.

Coming back to the conversation, Steven added: "But I think one must be more precise about which institutions one is talking about."

Reggie frowned thoughtfully. He poured another round. "Perhaps you're right. They say as one grows older, one appreciates change less."

They drank the next round in silence. Kitty caught Steven's eye as she emptied her glass. She stood up slowly. "Well, I'm off to bed, Reggie. Thanks very much for the champagne."

Reggie stood up immediately. Steven followed.

"I'm turning in myself, Reggie. And thanks." The Englishman looked crestfallen.

"I do hope we meet again. If not, here's my card. I could show you a bit of Istanbul the ordinary tourist doesn't see." He fumbled inside his waistcoat pocket and produced a visiting card.

Steven took it politely. "I'm sure. Thank you for your offer."

There was a knock on their compartment door as the train pulled out of the Budapest station.

"I wonder if it's that damn Reggie character," said Steven in a loud whisper.

"Well, if he's a spy, your kind of whisper won't do," Kitty retorted, her voice low. Steven got up from the breakfast they were taking in their sitting room and opened the door.

A gaunt, nervous-looking man with wire-rimmed glasses and a tick in one eye stood in front of him. "Herr Blauer?"

Steven caught his breath, then smiled and replied calmly. "Steven Blauer, you mean?"

"Yes. Yes. May I come in? I come from von Eschenberg."

Blauer, instantly pale, led the man in and shut the door behind him. He motioned the man to take a seat. "How is he?" said Steven, still standing and before the man could quite sit down.

"I have a letter for you," the man answered, taking an envelope out of his pocket.

Kitty stared at the scene before her, puzzled. Steven tore open the envelope and began to read:

My dear Stefan,

A dreadful decision has been made in the government. The worst element has won out. There will be war, dear Stefan. And it will be terrible. Already Jews and . . . my kind are being deported to camps by the trainload. Few people know this, but it is a fact.

I know about your journey. You must have realized now that the search for the Grail is in deadly earnest. Two lives have been lost in Montségur already.

I know that they have brandished my safety before you to keep you working for their evil—let me repeat, evil—ends. This can easily be remedied.

But as you read this letter, you should know that they no longer trust you. Your life is in danger, Stefan. Kriegshofer is saying that Miss Hammersmith is a Zionist spy, but I tell you, trust her. You must continue the quest. The Grail must never fall into their hands or all is lost. The atom, dear boy, the very fabric of the universe, will be in their hands.

You must follow your fate, Stefan, if for no other reason than to avenge your father's murder—yes, I have proof that they killed him. He had refused to help further.

You know the name Sebottendorf, I think. He is dead, some say murdered as well. Kriegshofer is now Reichsführer. Now you know all you need to know to act.

Find the Grail, Stefan. We are all depending on you. Safeguard it.

As for me, you are released, Stefan. I love you, as I loved your father, but with you, it is only your soul I have allowed myself to love. And that is right for this time and this place in eternity.

Farewell.

H. von Eschenberg.

Steven looked up from the letter, his face ashen, to face the gaunt man sitting in front of him.

"Is he dead?"

"Yes," the man replied quietly.

"By his own hand?"

"Yes."

"Thank God for that, then."

"Yes," replied the man, removing his glasses and rubbing his eyes wearily, "thank God for that."

After the man had left, Steven gave the letter to Kitty to read. She froze at the revelation of her role. She wondered how he would react.

"So that's it. I only have you, Kitty. I have no friend. I have no country." His voice was leaden; it frightened her, put her in a position in which she felt she had to make a commitment to Steven. She was not entirely ready to do that. One commitment seemed enough. But she actually wavered now. Their relationship had become so complicated. It was true that she had fallen in love with Steven, but since they'd begun the search for the Grail, she'd let the importance of the mission take precedence over everything else. It was, after all, what she'd set out to accomplish. And it was still of paramount importance to her.

"Who is Sebottendorf?" she asked at length.

"One of the SS who ordered this damned search."

"And his death?"

"Kriegshofer . . . a rival faction. It will be used for war."

"But how?" she asked incredulously. Blauer shrugged his shoulders. "Do you believe this business about atoms?" she continued.

"I must find the Grail before they do, Kitty. That's all I know. Dying men don't lie, especially men like Hans."

The train slowed as it neared the Rumanian frontier. They sat in silence in the sitting room of their compartment. Occasionally Steven pulled out a cigarillo, lit it, smoked it down to half, then put it out. Kitty watched him but said nothing: she respected his period of mourning.

The train screeched and jerked to an abrupt halt, throwing them partially out of their armchairs, knocking over the small dry bar. Whiskey spilled onto the burgundy carpet. Blauer jumped up and unlocked the compartment door and went out into the hall. Kitty stood up to follow, but hesitated. The corridor was filled with pressing bodies, passengers eager to find out what had happened. Idly she noticed that the whiskey spilled on the carpet created what might have been taken for a bloodstain. It grew as she watched it.

A woman's scream and then another followed.

Blauer was pushing through the crowd, and then suddenly was able to see out the window. Immediately his hand went for his pistol in the pocket of his jacket. It was the man from von Eschenberg, his body lacerated, decapitated beside the track. The sight horrified him so that he felt nothing, only numbness, then an urgent desire to get back to Kitty.

He shoved violently through the crowded corridor, decorum and manners no longer of any importance. Up ahead he thought he saw a man enter their compartment. It could have been another compartment, however. He gripped the gun. A man swore at him as he shoved him aside. He was almost at their suite.

Steven stood frozen at the entrance to the sitting room. A tall man with short-cropped blond hair and a thick, powerful neck stood in the middle of the room, his back to him.

Kitty's eyes betrayed Steven's presence. She was terrified.

The man whirled halfway around. "Blauer," he said.

Steven caught the silver glint of the man's gun as it turned toward him. Blauer fired once, then twice. The bull-necked man clutched his stomach. Blood spurted onto the carpet. His eyes rolled back into his skull, leaving only the whites.

Steven wrenched himself from the sight. "Kitty, take

this." He shoved her handbag into her arms. He took hold of the case containing his papers and money. "We're getting off the train." He pushed her gently ahead of him, out into the corridor and away from the man who now lay on the floor, spilling blood out of his half-opened mouth onto the carpet.

They climbed out of the train on the side opposite the remains of von Eschenberg's emissary. There was a grove of cypress in front of them, and low bushes. They could hide there.

Chapter Eight

The office of the new Reichsführer of the SS was elegantly modern and situated importantly on the Kaiser Wilhelm strasse. The oak-paneled walls and black SS banner darkened the room even at midday. Kriegshofer, especially during meetings, preferred it even darker and kept the drapes drawn. The orderly placed mid-morning coffee before each of the twelve men and Kriegshofer and then left the room.

Kriegshofer continued. "Do the Hungarian authorities suspect he is one of our men?"

"*Mein Reichsführer*, they do not even know Vebel is German. He carried no papers. His clothing had no labels." The officer betrayed his pride by speaking quickly, concisely and showing only seriousness and respect.

"You do your job with foresight, Strang. The Wehrmacht cannot complain of being *implicated* through one of their former officers." Kriegshofer's thin-lipped smile was brief. "But Blauer and the American woman are still alive."

"*But* the spy Laufendorf is quite dead," replied officer Strang.

"He was only von Eschenberg's courier. Of no importance. Blauer is still alive, and that is very important."

"You do not believe, *mein Reichsführer*, that he has any special—"

Häger at the end of the table coughed to interrupt. Kriegshofer, his face betraying anger at Strang's impertinence, smiled to the end of the table.

"Blauer obviously has a certain luck, Strang. He is still alive. And he is probably still heading for Istanbul. Fortunately the Turk Salamyurek will not be there to meet him. We are a step ahead, thanks to Berteil. And Vebel."

"A toast to the memory of Monsieur Berteil," grinned Kriegshofer, lifting his coffee cup. "And to a successful flight tomorrow morning." The others at the table raised their cups.

The Hotel Ozipek, from its top floors, overlooked the old city of Istanbul: the minarets of Ayasofya, the gardens of the Topkapi Museum, the Sublime Port and the Great Covered Bazaars, and beyond these to the Haliç, the Golden Horn to the north, the Bosporus to the east, the Sea of Marmara to the south. The view from the balcony of their suite could not have been more spectacular.

To avoid raising the slightest suspicion, Steven and Kitty had bought expensive European luggage in the Galata quarter of Istanbul before checking into the hotel. They had weighted the bags with carpets and brasses haggled for as briefly and politely as possible in the bazaar. Clothes were bought the following day in the same quarter.

After Svilengrad, they had slipped across the Turkish border at night, then backtracked partially to Adrianople to get the requisite visas from a Turkish official generous-minded enough to believe their story of having been lost on a hike when Blauer handed him a few large French bank notes along with the application forms. Glancing at the notes, he had then raised his eyes to Blauer and told him proudly that in the new Turkey, he would find all the modern conveniences. And at the Hotel Ozipek they had electric ceiling fans to keep the stifling late July air circulating in their rooms.

When they had checked into the hotel, they had taken the precaution of registering under Kitty's name in the hope of throwing off the track anyone trying to locate them in Istanbul. They had explained to the puzzled clerk checking their passport for the proper visas that they were on their honeymoon and preferred to remain incognito. A generous tip had helped him understand and forget Steven's real surname. Only afterward did they realize that few people in the hotel were registered under their true names; many of the wealthy Jews felt this more prudent. Istanbul was much too near the borders of the Reich for comfort. This factor in the end helped smooth the way for Kitty and Steven's ruse; it was commonplace and easily forgettable.

Yeniçeriler Cadessi, number 28, was not difficult to find by taxi, but getting free of the taxi driver was another matter. The taxi was unmetered, the fee had to be haggled over. Exasperated, Blauer, as the driver had hoped, finally thrust an absurdly large note into the man's gesticulating hand and got out. He arranged his suit, rumpled from the heat and dusty from the windowless ride, as best he could and pulled on the bell chain hanging beside a great wooden door cut in a windowless wall, marked 28.

An old woman swathed in black, but veilless in conformity with the new law, creaked open the door.

"Mr. Turgut Salamyurek?"

The woman shook her head: *"Burda degil, efendim."* Blauer stepped back and checked the number on the wall. It was correct.

"Yeniçeriler Cadessi?"

The woman smiled at his attempt at pronunciation and nodded. Blauer repeated the guide's name, and, again, the woman shook her head, but this time gestured for him to wait. She closed the door, leaving him still in the street.

Steven looked around him. The street was typically narrow and interspersed with shops which were merely large cubbyholes—doorless, windowless and able to be closed only by being bolted with great wooden shutters or—the more modern ones—by a corrugated iron shade. The neighborhood appeared neither rich nor poor, merely congested and old.

The woman reopened the door, smiled and gestured him inside. There he was in another world—cool, green with fig trees, refreshed by the gentle splashing of a mosaic fountain bubbling out of one wall into a small, shallow pool. She ushered him into the house, darkened against the midday sun, along a ceramic tiled loggia, half-shuttered, but one story up and overlooking the courtyard, until they reached an ornately carved door. She rapped on it, opened it, showed him in and shut the door behind him.

Blauer blinked, trying to adjust his eyes to the darkness of the room.

"Welcome, my friend," said a young man seated at a large table in a room which soon appeared to be a study of some kind. His English was nearly flawless. "My father has left Istanbul. May I help you?"

Blauer was unable to hide his confusion. "I wanted to hire his services as a guide."

"But precisely, sir. This is why my father is not in his home."

"When do you expect him back?"

"Surely not for a month at the least. I cannot be of

service? If it is to see the fabled Constantinople . . ."

"No, the Caucasus." The word seemed to explode in the room.

The young man got up suddenly from behind the table. "Who are you?"

Steven had no choice but to answer; Turgut Salamyurek was the key and at worst the end of his rope.

"Steven Blauer."

"You are German?"

Blauer hesitated. "Not exactly," he said truthfully. With von Eschenberg's death he had renounced his part in the Thousand Year Reich. He had not given up his German passport, but then technically he did not have one.

The young man eyed him with suspicion.

Blauer volunteered more information. "I was a German national. But now I am an American. I can show you my passport."

The young man smiled. "Passport?" He began to laugh. "Please do not take offense, sir. My name is Kemal. Three German gentleman hired my father's services to go to the Caucasus."

Blauer groaned audibly. Kemal looked at the tall, Germanic-looking man before him and suddenly he feared for his father's safety. He had not liked the three Germans.

"What do you know about this, Mr. Blauer?"

"I know . . ." Blauer's head swam for a second. "I know for one that your father is in danger of his life."

"They will kill him, won't they." Kemal's voice was steady.

"They may, when they get to their destination."

"Then . . ." Kemal's voice broke for a second. "My father is as good as dead, Mr. Blauer."

"There isn't a shorter route?"

"No."

"Can you take me there?"

Kemal's eyes seemed to glow in the darkened room. "Why?"

"For revenge." Blauer's words echoed in the room. Then there was silence. He could hear Kemal breathing.

"I will do it, by Allah." The young man's voice was a hiss.

Kitty did not particularly relish being alone, but she had little choice. Blauer had been gone a fortnight, no one linked with the rue des Rosiers had as yet contacted her and Istanbul was not a city conducive to an independent woman's idle pleasure-seeking, Atatürk or not. Shopping through the Grand Covered Bazaar alone, she saw few women—and these moved quickly through the alleyways between the shops—and the men either eyed her as a creature defiled or followed her to rub up against her, stroking their groins and whispering obscene demands in French or English in her ear.

Without Steven, she was trapped in Istanbul.

No one at the Hotel Ozipek came forth as a proper escort. The hotel was oddly empty of the usual kind of tourist, though it was completely booked with once-wealthy Jews waiting for ships to Haifa. Though she had never been there before, it was obvious that the Ozipek had been the equivalent of the famed Shepheard's in Cairo—a chic international stopover, a gathering spot for the local gentry, an institution of international exchange for those left in the world with money, power or both in common. Instead, the hotel was now somber, joyless, filled with anxious families smiling feebly at each other, hardly talking above whispers in the lounges and restaurants.

In mid-August Istanbul was stifling, a crossroad city holding its breath, waiting. Waiting for the little maniacal German with the funny mustache to make a

move, thought Kitty as she strolled for what seemed to
be the hundredth time through the Topkapi Gardens
to catch the breeze before sunset. And knowing what
that move would be did not exempt her from the tension of the wait.

As if for relief, she let her eye drift over the domes
of the former palace, then scan across the tall dark cy-
presses around her to catch the thrust of the minarets
of Hagia Sophia beyond.

Out of the corner of her eye, she thought she caught
the glint of metal. She looked around her. The part of
the gardens she had wandered into was still, seemingly
empty. She decided to turn back. A woman was a fool
to be so alone in Istanbul. She walked faster.

Other footsteps in the gravel besides her own made
her turn around suddenly. Kitty thought she caught a
movement: a branch of the cypress nearest her swayed
gently. Then the breeze reached her. She almost
laughed out loud. Her nerves were bristling; she
calmed them. She was ashamed of letting her imagination get the best of her.

She continued walking, then picked up speed. Prud-
ence did dictate that she return to the more populated
sections of the Topkapi. Despite her high heels she
soon found herself almost running along the gravel
path.

A low howl suddenly broke the stillness. Her nerves
wrenched her muscles into a run. The howl emerged
as a wail: the call of the muezzin to prayer. The sun
had set.

Her heart pounding, Kitty began to sob uncontroll-
ably as she ran. The image of the man lying in his
own blood in their parlor sitting room on the train
flashed before her. She was becoming hysterical; she
had to get a grip on herself. She forced her body to
slow down.

Out of the corner of her eye a metallic glint again
caught her attention. She hesitated, then turned

around. A crooked grin, a swarthy face, liquid black eyes, curly hair, the powerful, squat build of a man, a Turk, met her. He held a dagger calmly at his side. He grinned at her. The blade flashed in the dying light of the sun.

Kitty let out a little moan of fright. The man lunged forward suddenly, a low groan, a battle cry, erupting from his throat.

Kitty broke into a dead run. She was hobbled by her heels. The blade missed her side by half an inch, catching a fold of her dress, making a small rip.

She tried desperately to force a scream from her lungs as she ran. And then it came, loud and piercing. The Turk lunged forward again, missed her. Voices echoed in reply to her scream. A man in uniform rushed toward her, then another. Soon a crowd of people was around her. Her would-be assassin had vanished.

A woman with a little girl pointed to the rip in her chiffon dress and shook her head in commiseration: such a nice dress.

Kitty controlled her urge to laugh hysterically.

"Mrs. Blauer, isn't it? Whatever . . . My dear, you're dreadfully pale!" Kitty turned. It was Reggie, Reginald Cranston-Jones. Whatever she had thought of him before, she now fell against the stout Englishman and gripped his arm.

"Please! Get me out of here!"

One of the policemen who had given chase to the assassin now idled back, gesturing to the uniformed museum guards. The crowd talked heatedly. Amply fleshed Turkish women fanned themselves rapidly, anxiously twittering among themselves.

On Reginald Cranston-Jones's arm, Kitty stepped out of the Topkapi Garden into the Mur Adiye Hüda-vindicâr Cadessi, the street on which the Ozipek was located. In a silence imposed by Kitty's unvoiced will, they reached the entrance to the hotel.

Kitty turned to Reggie, pulled a cigarette out of her purse and lit it with a trembling hand, but she spoke with a calm which surprised her: "Let me buy us both a double whiskey."

Reggie broke into a smile, then a laugh. "You've got pluck, young lady."

The near-derelict steamer which left Istanbul to tramp from port to port along the Turkish coast of the Black Sea left them off at Rize, where the first peaks of the Caucasus loomed in the distance behind the ramshackle port. This first sea lap of their voyage had been especially slow: a Soviet coast guard boat had stopped the steamer almost as soon as it veered mistakenly beyond the forty-mile limit. They had searched the Turkish scow, seemingly looking for nothing in particular, but searched the boat thoroughly. The hashish-smoking, weathered Turk who captained the steamer shrugged his shoulders in resignation, then cursed the Russians foully as their coast-guard vessel steamed off.

The filthy atheists were looking for guns, he explained, guns for God-fearing men in the Ukraine. And then his anger vanished as he passed the thin hose of the nargileh to Kemal and then to Blauer, who only pretended to smoke the pungent hashish, billowing its smoke into the close air of the captain's cabin.

Kemal knew the old captain, because his father knew him. The young man could not have been a more ideal guide, Blauer had conceded very early on.

The early-morning breeze off the Black Sea sent a chill through them. But the air would soon be blisteringly hot as the sun rose higher. Steven stood at the rail next to Kemal as the town of Rize took on more detail as the boat neared the coast in the dawn haze.

Blauer wondered how much Kemal knew about the Grail, and how Kemal's father had ever become involved with it. He was a silent young man. They had not talked much.

Blauer turned to speak to Kemal, only to find him staring at him. "The men my father took to here, they were devils. Are you also a devil?" Kemal's face betrayed no emotion.

Steven laughed nervously. "I certainly hope not."

"It was my father's fate to be involved in this thing of Satan." Kemal paused, then looked back toward the town on the horizon.

"How did this happen, Kemal?"

The young Turk turned and eyed him with suspicion. Then he sighed and shrugged his shoulders. There was no point in remaining silent now.

"Many years ago, before I was born, a holy man came to my father with this thing. He knew that my father was a guide who knew the mountains, who knew places lost to most men. He asked my father to take him to such a place. My father agreed. Later the holy man told him that whoever came to him knowing that he was the guide to this place, my father should take him to it. My father believed the holy man to be a saint, a man of powers. My father used to say that the holy man had marked his life, had made him prosper while other guides remained poor.

"This is the devil's work, no? I think so, Mr. Blauer." Kemal searched Steven's face. "But I do not think you are a devil. I think you were the man whom my father was to lead to the village. So I am my father's son and I am taking you to the village, by Allah." Kemal began to laugh suddenly, a hard, bitter laugh. "But perhaps the men of the mountains, the bandits who rule where the government army does not dare go, perhaps they will kill them. Perhaps they will kill us. And that will be the end of this devil thing. It will be lost and forgotten."

"Lost, perhaps, Kemal. But I doubt if it will be forgotten."

Kemal's laughter ceased abruptly. He turned his gaze once more to the shoreline. "Yes, you are wise. You were the man."

A silence fell over them, as if the shore and the mountains beyond had reached out and possessed them with the foreboding of a prophetic dream.

Within an hour of debarkation at Rize, Kemal and Blauer were seated sipping raki in a sailor's café.

"My father has passed through here," announced Kemal, retaking his seat after leaving the outdoor table and going into the bar. "It was more than a fortnight ago. It is hopeless."

"He was with the three Germans?"

"He was with the three Germans." Kemal took a sip of the harsh, milky-colored liquor.

"Then it will be revenge after all," said Blauer quietly after several minutes of silence.

"Yes, for revenge." Kemal drained his glass. "Tonight we sleep in Rize in the house where we will get the horses and equipment." Kemal stood up from the small wooden table. For a moment he seemed frozen as he looked beyond the tangle of telegraph lines ringing the back foothills of the town and off into the cold purple peaks beyond.

Blauer followed Kemal's gaze, then stood up. "Let's go then. We need a solid night's sleep on dry land."

Kemal turned back to Steven. There were tears welling in the young Turk's eyes.

The trip through the mountain passes was arduous. The twists of the trails kept them inching forward into the interior. Near the summits the air grew thin, making it difficult for the horses and for them to breathe, exhausting them prematurely. Days passed. The splendor of the Caucasus paled from their exhaustion. But they were not stopped or attacked by bandits, which surprised Kemal. He had expected some kind of encounter and had brought articles of gold to appease them as his father always did.

And then on the tenth day they knew why.

At the side of a trail, sloping down off the side of one of the peaks, lay six bullet-ridden bodies, some with skulls shattered, others with their broad bright-patterned sashes and pantaloons stained reddish-brown with dried blood.

"They have machine guns," said Blauer quietly.

Kemal blinked nervously, then prodded the horses on down the slope.

That night they camped in a large cave in which they could also hide the horses.

"If God wills, we shall be at the village tomorrow." Kemal took a swig out of the leather water bag and handed it to Blauer. The night was moonless. They could not see beyond the immediate range of the campfire they had made at the mouth of the cave.

Blauer stared out at the blackness and drank. Beads of perspiration were on his forehead, but the night was cold. He wiped them off with the back of his hand.

"I'm feeling sick, Kemal."

"How is it?" The young Turk licked his lips nervously.

"Odd. A kind of fever, nausea."

Kemal nodded. "I feel it too, my friend." They stared at each other for a moment.

After a while Steven said: "What is it?"

"It is different. Very different. I don't know." Kemal got up and began kicking dirt on the fire. "We must sleep." They moved into the back of the cave and rolled up in their blankets on the ground.

At first Blauer could not sleep, exhausted as he was. He had no idea what he would find tomorrow in the village; he had no plan. They had brought guns, but not machine guns. They would have to approach the village with caution.

And then his exhaustion took him over so that he lay tensed on the edge of sleep, neither awake nor asleep. He lay for hours or minutes like this—he could not tell which.

A moaning sound brought him to his feet. Branches cracked underfoot. The moan turned into a singsong, then a long spasm of coughing. Kemal sat up abruptly, reaching for his rifle. Steven already had his pocket revolver in his hand.

Kemal yelled out into the darkness in Turkish. A frightened voice answered. Kemal spoke again. Out of the blackness came a figure dragging one leg. Blauer struck a match. He stepped back, a cry of horror caught in his throat. One side of the face of the young man edging toward them was a molten-looking mass of red flesh. There was no left eye, no left ear.

"What's happened to the poor devil?"

Kemal questioned the man.

"He makes no sense. He talks about God shaking the mountains, the sky becoming fire. I don't know."

"The fire part would explain his face."

The disfigured mouth of the young man spluttered a few words of Turkish.

"He wants water," said Kemal finally, after he had made the man repeat his request several times over.

Suddenly the man fell to his knees before them. A repulsive gurgling sound came out of his throat, a blackish liquid dribbled from his mouth, and then he fell forward on his face.

Blauer rushed forward, then stopped over the man. He was afraid to touch him. He turned him over on his back with one foot, then crouched and held his palm an inch over the man's mouth and nose.

"He's dead, Kemal."

"God give him peace."

Rather than touch the body, Blauer insisted on leaving it. He was relying on nothing more than a vague intuition of contamination from it; they moved out of the cave and slept in the open.

Dawn woke them early. Blauer had not slept well. He still felt nauseous, but fortunately he had not vomited and lost strength. He looked back at the body in the cave, then struggled to his feet. He looked eastward toward the rising sun.

"My God, look! Oh my God!"

Kemal jumped to his feet, then followed Blauer's gaze. The east was black with smoke. The sun broke through the haze, only to turn the sky bloody.

"That is the direction of the village," said Kemal quietly.

They breakfasted in silence on jerkied meat and water. Blauer held it down with difficulty. They set off within the hour.

The smoke in the east seemed to abate as the day progressed. The forest fire—or so they could only conceive of the awful holocaust as being—was going out, stopped most likely by snowy slopes.

But nothing had prepared them for what lay before them as they rounded the last mountain before the village and stood looking into the valley. Where the village had once stood, a huge charred crater gaped before them.

"They found it," said Blauer. His mind raced. He remembered Sebottendorf's words, then Kriegshofer's concerning the power of the Grail. The meeting at Vogelsang seemed centuries away; there before them lay the new order.

Blauer shuddered, unable to stop himself for what seemed like hours. The nausea and fever had been radiation poisoning: were they both doomed? Kemal stood staring into the blackened pit of the valley, unable to comprehend, unable to speak.

And then suddenly Blauer took heart. "Perhaps the three Germans have been killed in the blast. It is our only hope."

Kemal frowned, then spoke finally: "This you call hope, my friend?" He shook his head.

Blauer touched the young Turk's shoulder. "No, Kemal. No. It is the Germans who have done this. They have learned from the Grail. We must hope that what they have learned has died with them."

Kemal shook his head: "God has done this, not men, not the Germans." He sank to his knees and began the Muslim prayers, knocking his head hard against the earth.

Blauer stood over him motionless, lost in thoughts of his father, respectful of Kemal's piety. Gerd Blauer had known about this; he had kept the knowledge from them as long as he could, and then they had killed him. Now it was up to him.

He shuddered again. He looked across the valley to the unscarred mountains beyond. All at once it seemed familiar. He shook his head. He could not place it immediately, and then suddenly he knew: the Pog, the ruined fortress of Monsalvat. That's what it looked like. He smiled to himself. He had indeed come a long way.

Kemal finished his prayers and stood up. His forehead was bleeding slightly, but he paid no mind to it.

"Let's skirt the valley," said Blauer.

Kemal nodded. They left the horses tethered there and headed off on foot. Their search was short. They found tracks of boots and horses. They were fresh and led out of the valley west and north.

"God save us," said Blauer quietly. The SS had left, the Grail in their hands; the Phoenix Formula in their minds.

Chapter Nine

It was Olga Bartok who had decided on the ramshackle rooms overhanging the fetid waters of the Haliç, as if ready to tumble down into them. She had overridden Silver's objections by pointing out that the area was a perfect rabbit warren of alleys and structures built one on top of another, following no plan but the law of gravity. Reluctantly he had had to agree. It would be a perfect hideout when the time came.

So it was settled, and she would stay there herself. When he had met her as prearranged in the café Le Bosphore, Silver had, after a few moments' conversation, decided that she was mad as a hatter. She was not a Jew. Her involvement in the mission seemed to come from some bizarre mysticism. Yet he knew that the people in Paris who had sent her to him were thorough realists, pragmatists. And as she talked further, he had to respect her fanatical dedication to securing the Grail—a dedication placed at their disposal. If she chose to live in such surroundings, so be it.

Olga laughed now as she remembered Silver's snobbish look of disgust. How could such a *petit bourgeois* ever understand the indifference of a noblewoman who had been raised in castles and grand hotels to such surroundings? Not only were they practical, but they suited her mood. She no longer had the patience for the social chitchat which would have inevitably been necessary had she put up at a good European-style hotel. She preferred the freedom of the native quarter, a freedom she could never have enjoyed in so-called respectable surroundings.

With a muffled grunting sound the naked young Turkish man beside her turned away. Her eye examined appreciatively the tight muscles of his body, his round arms and legs, his hard, young buttocks. The part of his anatomy she appreciated most was now hidden from view. She smiled to herself.

He had claimed to be nineteen. She figured he couldn't be a day over fifteen. Boys became men early in Oriental climates. And they cost a good deal less than their Parisian counterparts.

A sigh of pleasure escaped from her lips. She liked paying for sex, she realized. It gave her a heady sense of power. And, she noted practically, how else could an old woman expect to attract a young man to her bed?

Kitty Hammersmith lit a Turkish cigarette as she waited for Reggie to come up in the elevator. The ennui of the stay in Istanbul while waiting for Blauer's return had taken her from an occasional after-dinner cigarette to a nearly chain-smoking habit. Her brush with death in the Topkapi Gardens had accelerated the addiction.

More than a week had passed since the incident. She no longer walked in the gardens or anywhere else in the streets of Istanbul except with Reggie. She had become a virtual prisoner in her suite at the Hotel Ozipek.

The expected knock on the door came. Kitty rose slowly, walked over and opened it.

"Hello, my dear. Sleep well?" Reggie strode into the room. She smiled. She still found his jolly roundness amusing.

"Oh, not bad." She took a puff on her cigarette, shutting the door and reentering the comfortably appointed sitting room with its Turkish carpets, marble floors and heavy, carved Turkish divans and armchairs. The french doors onto the balcony were open so that the fine gauze curtains fluttered in off the Bosporus.

Kitty caught Reggie eyeing her appreciatively. She walked over to an end table and put her cigarette out in a modern shell-shaped silver ashtray she had picked up in one of the European shops in Galata.

"Where shall it be today then, my dear Mrs. Blauer?" Kitty frowned. "Nothing's wrong, I hope. No nasty visitors?" he added, plopping his full weight down on the divan so that the springs twanged softly. "Have you heard from your husband, Kitty?"

She went to her purse on the writing table near the window and took another cigarette out of the pack, lit it and sat down in the armchair facing the divan. Not only had she heard nothing from Steven, her contact from the man on the rue des Rosiers had never materialized.

"No, nothing. Not a word from him."

"My, my . . . What do you think is holding him up?"

Kitty had told Reggie that Steven had insisted on taking an overland tour into Cappadocia, but that the trip was considered too harsh for a woman and so she had been left behind.

"I hope nothing critical. He did mention the possibility of running into bandits."

Reggie made a clucking sound of disapproval but said nothing. Then his face brightened.

"I have it. I know this marvelous little seafood restaurant a little beyond Üsküdar. Let's have lunch in Asia, my dear."

Kitty laughed. "All right. Let's go immediately, then." She stood and picked up her purse from the table. She turned toward Reggie. He had not moved. She caught him with his face creased in thought. She had never seen the jovial Englishman like this before.

Suddenly she wondered if she had not been too rash in bringing him into her life simply because he happened to have been her accidental savior in the Topkapi. She really knew only the surface of him, nothing more, and that had seemed amusing enough up until that moment.

His face brightened into a smile the second he felt her eyes on him. He got up with a melodramatic groan of exertion.

"What were you just thinking of, Reggie? I've never seen you so serious," she said as he opened the door for her.

"Oh, whether I should tell you something."

She stopped in her tracks. She had expected a quip in reply, not a frank statement.

"What did you decide?"

"That I'd tell you over lunch. Come on, my dear. The berlin motorcar is waiting downstairs. I hope Ahmed turned off the motor to save petrol."

Istanbul was periodically plagued by shortages of one thing or another. Some said it was the signs of the prelude to war: stockpiling.

The large Mercedes-Benz maneuvered through the crowded tangle of streets toward the ferry that would take them across the Bosporus from Europe to Asia. Already it was the third of September. A cooler breeze now swept almost constantly over the dense city.

They left the car with Ahmed in the bowels of the ferry and went topside to catch the late-morning sun and the full wind over the water. Reggie was still dressed in his summer whites, replete with Panama hat, which he now doffed to mop his moist brow with a large blue polka-dot silk handkerchief. Kitty leaned against the railing and looked down into the churning water of the Bosporus. For a split second fear gripped her totally—fear for Steven, fear for herself—and then she overcame it. She looked across the water at the small boats scurrying from one shore to another, their brightly colored sails full with wind. Large steamers moved slowly on toward the Black Sea or down to the Mediterranean.

"What were you planning to say to me?" she said suddenly, turning to Reggie.

He laughed heartily. "Now that would be telling. It's nothing that can't wait for lunchtime. You should be a master at the art of patience, my dear young lady, shouldn't you?"

Kitty shrugged her shoulders and looked back out over the harbor.

"I don't know what I'll do if something has happened to Steven." The words seemed to have broken free of her on their own. She was a bit startled by their intensity.

"Absence makes the heart grow fonder. A cliché, perhaps, my dear," said Reggie, patting her on the arm, "but very, very true."

"I love him." She stood up straight, adjusting the shoulder pads which gave the wide, sturdy look to women's clothes, all the fashion now. She had ceased being shocked by these three words; she was totally in love with Blauer. If she had ever doubted it, his first week away from her had made it obvious. She longed for the feel of his body, for his breath on her cheek, his tenderness, the sound of his voice—everything.

She had not bargained on that. She had turned out to be a fool of a Mata Hari.

"What's the matter now, Kitty? You *are* in quite a stew this morning, aren't you?"

"It's been over a month."

Reggie nodded in understanding.

"Let's get back down to the car."

The berlin left the ferry and skirted the shoreline with its ramshackle houses poised as if ready to fall into the water at any moment. Soon they motored past beaches still flocked with bathers, under pines which shaded the route, until the car stopped in front of a modest-looking restaurant adjacent to one of the beaches.

The Turkish host, garbed in sash and pantaloons, came out to the car himself and opened the door.

"Efendim," he bowed to Reggie. "Madame," he added as Kitty got out first, followed by a puffing Reggie.

"My usual table, Ismet."

The swarthy, large-bellied Turk swept one arm toward the entrance of the restaurant. They passed through a small dark area honeycombed with kitchen and washroom and living quarters, out onto a terrace hanging over the sea and into the blazing sun. The terrace was nearly empty. Ismet clapped and a boy ran out. He gave a command, and soon the awning was stretched out to shade Reggie's table from the noon sun. The table was right at the edge of the terrace. From one side the coast curved sharply, and the great expanse of the Black Sea could be seen in the distance.

In the back of the restaurant, probably from the kitchen, came the sound of a radio wailing forth harsh, rhythmic Turkish popular songs.

"Let me order for us," said Reggie, settling into his seat.

Kitty placed her purse under her chair, the table being too small to accommodate it and their meal.

Ismet came to take their order.

"My digestion is in your hands, Reggie," Kitty

laughed as the two men conspired over the menu in Turkish.

Ismet was pleased with the choices, curling his broad mustache in sign of it, then bowed and left. In a moment the boy appeared with a carafe of raki, glasses, water and ice. Reggie poured for both of them, then raised his apéritif in a wordless toast. Kitty touched his glass with hers.

First vegetable salads arrived, creamed cucumbers, tomatoes and onions and chickpeas. Then came stuffed vine leaves, and then the fish—a large red mullet stuffed with rice and spices and olives with a thick sesame sauce. Kitty ate sparingly but with relish of the enormous luncheon. Reggie consumed the rest, along with mouthfuls of harsh red wine.

Suddenly the background blare and crackle of the music on the radio was interrupted by the voice of an announcer. He sounded breathless. Reggie put down his knife and fork and stopped chewing, listening intently. He swallowed and put his finger to his lips to stop Kitty from questioning him. And then the music resumed.

"What was that all about?" Kitty was grinning, but Reggie's expression was hard, grim.

"Herr Hitler has invaded Poland." The two of them stared at each other for a moment.

"So at last it has come," said Kitty slowly.

"Not so surprising, is it?" Reggie had lost interest in the meal. He tapped the white tablecloth nervously with his fingers.

"No, I suppose not."

"And, of course," he began slowly, staring at Kitty intently, "it means they found it."

Kitty tensed immediately. "Found what, Reggie?"

He laughed quietly: "Let's not play cat and mouse, my dear. That Grail thing, of course. Those in Berlin who wanted war in order to begin their plan for the world, their extermination plans, would not have made such a move without knowing that they had the ultimate weapon in their hands."

Kitty stared at Reggie in disbelief. "Who are you, Reggie?"

"Well, my dear, to begin with, not Reggie. I'm afraid Silver is the name, Jonathan Silver. Mean anything to you?"

"No."

"It's Jewish, my dear. What is Hammersmith?" Kitty, annoyed at his tone, started up from the table. "Don't forget your purse under your chair, my dear, if you do insist on leaving, though I don't think you will. I'm your contact. Rue des Rosiers." Kitty sat down.

"Oh," she said. She could not think of anything else to say.

"I've been in Palestine. A messy business, Palestine. Soon to get messier."

"You aren't one of the . . . ?"

"A terrorist, one of those Zionist hoodlums the press has a fieldday with? Well, what do you call yourself, Miss Hammersmith?"

"Hardly a terrorist."

"An abettor of terrorism? A Zionist sympathizer?"

"A sympathizer, yes. For freedom, for justice . . ."

Reggie broke into uproarious laughter.

Kitty reached for her purse and put it in front of her on the table. "Take me back to the hotel, please."

"Ah, but you haven't had your dessert, my dear. Ismet's baklava is a delight."

"I'm not hungry. Please take me back."

Reggie clapped his hands. Ismet rushed out onto the terrace.

"The check, Ismet. It was superb."

"Something is wrong, *efendim*. No cakes? No baklava?"

"The lady is not hungry."

"Ah, it is the news on the wireless. I am sorry, very

sorry. You are touched? I am truly sorry." He bowed and handed Reggie the bill, which he promptly paid.

"You are too generous, *efendim*. Come again. Come again, lady. Come when the news is more pleasant."

"I'm afraid that would make for a long absence," replied Kitty unexpectedly. The two men blinked.

"Come again in any case, lady. Thank you," bowed Ismet.

They went to the car and got in. Ahmed started the motor, and they began their drive back to the Hotel Ozipek in silence.

As they entered the suburb of Üsküdar, Kitty turned to Jonathan Silver, alias Reggie Cranston-Jones.

"Is that what you were debating telling me?"

"What, my dear?"

"That you were my contact?"

"That was part of it."

"What was the rest, then?"

He paused, then looked away from her out the window. "We'll be at the ferry soon. I should rather speak to you in private, perferably in your rooms, if you'll permit that."

Kitty sighed: "Why shouldn't I?"

The breeze had dropped off. The room had grown close and had darkened with the sinking of the sun toward the west. Kitty put out her cigarette and stood up.

"No," she said in a strained voice, "you don't believe me; I don't believe you." She glanced at her wrist-watch, then walked over to the dry bar set up beneath the mirror that stretched along one length of wall. "But I will mix you a drink. I'm having a dry martini."

Reggie—she had decided still to call him that; she did not like his real name—mopped the perspiration

from his forehead with his blue polka-dot handkerchief. His white suit was severely wrinkled now. He
looked awful, she thought as she stared at him, waiting
for his answer.

"I'll have the same."

Kitty mixed a pitcher of martinis, poured two and
brought them to Reggie. She handed him his and immediately took a sip of her own. She stood for a moment, not wanting to sit down and recommence the
argument, the pressure. She could, of course, ask him to
leave, but what if he were right, or what if Steven were
dead? In any case she had volunteered for this little bit
of espionage, she had given her word. Her word meant
a great deal to her now; she figured it was about all
she had going for her in the world.

Then she remembered her father, her real father,
and felt ashamed of herself. He had put up with so
much more. She was rich; most people were not. She
went to the big, ornate divan and sat down. She lit
another cigarette, then took a sip of her drink. She felt
Reggie's eyes on her. She looked up. He was staring at
her.

"What can I say to convince you, my dear?"

"Nothing."

"But surely—" he began, then stopped. "Did you see
Blauer leave with the guide?"

"No," she sighed in reply.

"So he could have been lying. He could have gone
off with this Turgut character, with the father; he
could have made the whole damn thing up."

"Why?"

"To throw you off the track, of course."

"I can't for the life of me figure why he would do
that," she replied sarcastically.

"Because he is using you as he has used you in the
past."

"I told you about the letter," she said wearily,
"about his friend von Eschenberg. Believe me, he has

changed. He is changed. They killed his father and his father's best—"

"His lover?" smiled Reggie.

"Yes, his lover! What of it?" She was angry now. Reggie backed off. He sipped his martini slowly. Kitty bolted hers, got up and poured herself another. She sat down again, took a final puff on her cigarette and put it out. After a few sips of her freshened drink, she lit another.

Time was on his side. Reggie turned away to hide his smile from her.

"All right," he sighed dramatically. "Let us suppose you are right. Let us—"

Her expression became fierce instantly. "I *am* right!" She realized that she was feeling the alcohol but continued to sip her martini. "They tried to kill us, didn't they?"

"All right, my dear. Granted. Supposing then that Blauer is, shall we say, neutral. You are not going to tell me now that he has gone from being a Nazi to being a Zionist?"

"Who's a Zionist?"

"*You* are, for one, my dear Kitty. And so am I."

"Well, for your information, I am not a Zionist. Why should I be? I'm not a Jew. I don't give a damn for some silly Biblical Promised Land, some crazy Israel. I'm in this because I care for human life." Her face was flushed, her breathing harsh and fast.

"A bit of calm, my dear, *really*." His smile was maddening.

"Get the hell out of here! I'm finished with all of you." She jumped to her feet but Reggie stayed put.

He shook his head slowly from side to side. "Please sit down, Kitty. This is getting us both nowhere."

Kitty looked down at the carpet. She had spilled her martini. Instantly she recalled the stain on the floor of the parlor suite in the train, then the blood. She picked up the glass from the carpet and stood up straight, feeling a bit dizzy. She took the glass to the bar and refilled it.

"As I was saying, Kitty." His voice was soft. "Blauer is a neutral in this matter. But he is also alone, exposed. Suppose he does have the Grail. Suppose he comes back to Istanbul with it. How long do you think it will be before they catch up with him, kill him and take it?"

Kitty made no reply. Her face was expressionless.

"By your being with us when he returns, reading the, well, the kipnapping note we shall leave, he will hand the Grail over to us." He stopped to wait for some response from her.

Kitty was staring at her lap, into the goblet of the martini, as if mesmerized by the liquid. He went on: "Surely you agree that it is far better for us to have the Grail in our possession than the Nazis. We have the power to *keep it safe!* Blauer does not."

Kitty looked up finally. Her face was studiedly amused. "You don't believe in this Grail nonsense, do you?"

From her voice, Reggie could tell that she was drunk. "Gerd Blauer did, my dear Kitty. Steven's father believed in it, was deadly serious about its powers and was about to turn it over to us when they *killed* him."

Kitty's eyes widened suddenly. Her smirk vanished.

The air stank of sewerage from the Haliç, the Golden Horn of Byzantium. And where there was sewerage along the waterfront, there were rats, thought Kitty as she followed Reggie up the stairs of the sagging wooden structure hanging perilously over the water. The stone steps were slippery with accumulated slime. It was dark now. A rat could scamper across her path, or worse, and she would not know until she felt it.

They reached the top of the stairs. Reggie, ahead of

her, was panting heavily. From the distance came the lowing of the tugboats and the ubiquitous radio music, wailing harshly amidst the clatter of slum kitchens, the odor of garlic, frying onions and olive oil. The cooking smells mixed in the night air with the stench of the Haliç and made her slightly nauseous.

Reggie rapped on the door in what appeared to be a code of some kind. Latches were undone, bolts drawn and then the door creaked open; letting a shaft of light into the stairwell which blinded them for a moment.

"Is she with you?" asked a woman's voice. Kitty found it vaguely familiar.

"Yes," replied Reggie with triumph. He hoisted himself up the final stair.

"Splendid."

Reggie turned toward Kitty. "Come on, my dear. You're among friends."

Kitty followed Reggie into the room. It was not as brightly lit as she had thought, but it took a moment for her to adjust her eyes to it. Then she saw the woman.

"I know you, don't I?" Kitty stared at her. The woman was distinctly familiar, but she could not place her.

"You have a poor memory, Kitty."

Then Kitty knew. "Not so poor, Countess."

Olga Bartok straightened haughtily. Kitty's tone was mocking. "You are not obliged to use my title. But it *is* mine, I can assure you."

Reggie interrupted with a loud laugh. "You're succeeding in proving that the female of the species is nothing but cats. Come, come now, ladies. You do yourselves an injustice."

"I apologize," Kitty said immediately, "if I have said anything to offend you, Madame Bartok."

Olga Bartok nodded, then turned to Reggie. "Some interesting news has come to us."

Reggie was still breathing heavily. He took out his handkerchief and wiped his face. "I'm sure it is something I shall want to be seated for." He looked around for a chair.

The room was small. In the middle was a table. Along one wall beneath a minuscule window was a low cot. A naked light bulb hung down from the low ceiling over the table. Back in one corner was a none-too-sturdy-looking chair.

Reggie's eyes returned to the cot. "Shall we sit down over there?"

"You may sit, Silver. I prefer to stand. Perhaps Miss Hammersmith prefers to sit as well."

"I do, yes," said Kitty, following Reggie to the cot. Before sitting down she turned to Olga Bartok: "But if all this kidnapping business is necessary, couldn't we at least have better quarters?"

Olga laughed. Reggie coughed.

"Better quarters are much more conspicuous, Miss Hammersmith. As you well know, money is always conspicuous."

At first Kitty took the remark as an insult, then laughed. Madame Bartok, if she was truly an aristocrat as she claimed, understood all too well. She began to feel some sympathy for the woman. After all, she had lost everything.

"Are you a Jew?" Kitty asked suddenly.

"That depends on whom you consult," replied Olga dryly. "The Nazis considered me as such—there is some mixing of blood on the Hungarian side back several generations—it was more expedient for the bloodsuckers in Vienna to consider me a Jew. They made a considerable fortune off of it, I am told."

"What was this news?" interrupted Reggie. "You two will have plenty of time to chat. I must get back."

Olga turned to Reggie. It was obvious that she was not accustomed to being interrupted, and, in addition, did not have much respect for Reggie's sense of irony.

"Oh, my dear Silver, I'm sure terrorism can wait a few hours more, can it not?"

"You're nothing but a damned anti-Semite," he exploded. Kitty was startled by his vehemence.

"Perhaps I am," replied Olga Bartok coldly.

Reggie visibly backed off. For a few moments silence filled the room while tempers cooled.

"There is word from Rize," she began.

Reggie sat up. "And . . . ?"

"It seems there was a devastating earthquake or something of the kind in the interior—in the mountains, not far from Lake Van."

Reggie sucked in his breath. "Then it's true."

"It would seem so. Gerd Blauer was no liar, Silver. He was no liar indeed," Olga Bartok added slowly.

Kitty found it hard to follow. "What's true?" interrupted Kitty. She pulled a cigarette out of her purse and put it to her lips.

"What they are calling an earthquake, my dear, was no such thing. It was manmade. The Grail contains that information—among other things. Among better, more constructive things." Olga Bartok stopped speaking. She seemed to have forgotten both Kitty and Reggie for the moment. Her mind was elsewhere.

Kitty was reminded of the palm-reading sequence in the train. Perhaps it had not been a sham.

"Gerd Blauer was my friend," Olga said suddenly. Her eyes glistened. "His son needs our protection."

Chapter Ten

Just before dawn on the tenth of August, an unmarked airplane had received clearance from the flight tower at Berlin's Templehof Field. Within minutes of takeoff it had attained an unusually high altitude and then had marked a course due south and east. A thickly curtained black Mercedes-Benz limousine had immediately driven off the field and headed north toward the Kaiser Wilhelm Strasse.

That morning visitors who had appointments with the Reichsführer of the SS were surprised to find them canceled until further notice. Herr Kriegshofer, Herr Strang and Herr Häger were announced to have gone on a tour of inspection. It was leaked later that it was to be a lightning visit to Krössinsee, Vogelsang and Sonthofen. The leak was met with admiration, tinged with fear: the new Reichsführer was implacably demanding.

The unmarked aircraft had landed at a private airfield not far from Uzun-Kopru in European Turkey. A Rolls-Royce Silver Shadow had met the three stylishly dressed men and whisked them in ostentatious luxury through the Turkish countryside to Istanbul. They put up in a private mansion on the outskirts of

Galata. The following day they made a visit to Yen-içeriler Cadessi, 28.

Now their successful journey was nearing an end. Below them lay the town of Rize, nestled into the coast at the foot of the Caucasus Mountains. From there Kriegshofer would telegraph the code to Wilhelmstrasse that would free the Führer to win over Stalin with that ultimate argument which was the Phoenix Formula, and invade Poland.

As arduous as the return through the mountains had been—they were short on food—the three Germans were constantly ecstatic. They had told stories around the campfire of the early days in Munich and Stuttgart, passing around the bottle of good schnapps which Herr Häger had had the good sense to bring along from Berlin. And they toasted their guide. Turgut Salamyurek drank with them, a modest smile of thanks on his face. Wisdom counseled keeping a generous smile in the direction of the devil.

The machine gunning had been horrific enough, but the blasting of the village into hell had frozen his heart in his chest. A nauseating fluid had seemed to replace the blood in his veins. And it was still that which flowed in him.

He wished in his heart that he had never seen the holy man, the German named Gerd Blauer. He cursed him wherever he was. And he doubly cursed the thing, the devil's instrument, which lay secreted in Kriegshofer's saddlebags.

Turgut Salamyurek knew after the destruction of the village that his life was worth only the trip back through the mountains to Rize. Herr Strang kept his machine gun constantly hanging by its strap from his shoulder. If he did not keep it pointed directly at their excellent Turkish guide, it was only because it was unnecessary.

So Turgut Salamyurek would do what any self-respecting Turk would do; he would sacrifice his life for a purpose. He would lose them all hopelessly in the mountains, lose himself as well so that under torture he could not be forced back on the right trail to Rize. But he had not bargained on Strang. The German's memory for geographical detail was more than extraordinary: it was satanic. When they were an hour off the trail, he had called the guide to his side, smiling broadly at him. The old man's heart had turned to ice.

"You took the wrong path back where the rock breaks out of the ground in the shape of a finger, my friend." Strang had shaken his head slowly, the broad smile firmly fixed on his face.

Turgut Salamyurek had grinned back, then bowed, shaking his head from side to side. "I am a man growing old, *efendim*. You are right. But we are not far off."

"No, we are not," Strang had replied, still smiling. Now Rize lay before them in the distance.

Without looking at the three Germans, he knelt on the ground, facing south away from the Black Sea and toward Mecca, and began his prayers. It was not particularly the right time of day for prayer, but that no longer mattered.

As Turgut Salamyurek's forehead lay pressed for a moment against the cool, moist earth, Strang pointed the machine gun at the old man's head and shattered it with a burst of gunfire so that it lay open like a broken watermelon.

Steven Blauer had parted from Kemal Salamyurek as soon as they had debarked from the Black Sea steamer. They had shaken hands warmly, and Kemal with tears in his eyes had kissed Blauer in the Turkish fashion.

The body of Turgut Salamyurek had been found in the mountains by woodcutters from Rize. It had been identified at first by papers on the body, then with a cry of anguish by the owner of the waterfront café which the old guide had always frequented when in Rize. A few days later Kemal and Blauer had entered the town.

Blauer had paid for a funeral, replete with professional mourners and a band, which had only been seen in Rize when Mehmed Pasha, the biggest landowner and shipper in the region, had died ten years before.

Now Blauer was glad, if somewhat fearful, to return to the Hotel Ozipek. He remembered vaguely that someone early on in his quest had said that with the Grail and Germany lay a universal conflict unlike anything the world had seen in millennia: a war of good against evil. He no longer found these words extraordinary or overblown; they did not even begin to do justice to the situation, to what he had witnessed in the mountains. And now like a child he again believed wholeheartedly in the devil.

If only he could believe as surely in God.

"Is Mrs. Hammersmith in?"

The desk clerk shook his head. "I'm afraid not, Mr. Hammersmith. We have not seen her for a few days now." Steven turned pale. "I hope there is nothing wrong, Mr. Hammersmith."

"No. No. No, certainly. She had no idea when I'd be back. I'll just go up." Steven took the key from the clerk and went to the elevator.

He was shaken with a feeling of foreboding as the elevator let him out at the top floor. He found their suite and let himself in.

"Kitty?" His voice seemed to echo in the entry, then, as he repeated her name, in the sitting room, then in the bedroom. She was not there. He tried to calm himself. There was no reason in particular why she should be there waiting for him like some Penelope at her loom.

He went back into the sitting room and removed his

jacket. The small revolver in the pocket made the coat slump into a heap on the divan. In his waistcoat and shirtsleeves he sank down beside it on the heavy, ornate divan.

He looked about the room. Everything was in order; no signs of struggle.

A rap on the door made him start in his seat. He was distinctly on edge: he did not like the look of things, but he did not know of what in particular. He got up and opened the door. It was the porter with his luggage, which had been sent on from the port. He directed the man toward the bedroom and went over to the dry bar. He needed a drink. Idly he mixed a whiskey and water, then tipped the porter as the man crossed the sitting room to let himself out.

"Would you open the french doors before you leave, please?" he ordered, pointing toward the balcony. The man bowed and opened the doors. The room had been unbearably close, airless. Now the gauze curtain rippled in the breeze off the Bosporus.

"Thank you, please, *efendim*," said the porter, bowing his way out of the suite and shutting the door firmly behind him.

The previous tomblike staleness of the air had reminded Steven unpleasantly of Vogelsang. Many things did now. His dreams were haunted by the specters of Kriegshofer, round tables, red-white-and-black swastika banners and the sight of craters in the earth and bullet-riddled bodies.

He had failed. He had failed his father. He had failed the unsuspecting world; in Rize he had learned of the Polish campaign. Rumors of atrocities perpetrated on Polish peasants, clergy, aristocracy and Jews were rampant, along with news of the blitzkrieg. Knowing the Grail was in their possession, his countrymen, the SS, had unleashed their arrogance, their hatred.

He walked back to the divan, lost in thought, and sat down. His eyes were on his feet as he mulled over the events of the past few months. How could he have ever guessed? In fairness, he could not really berate himself for not having believed in the Grail. Who in their right mind would believe in anything so fantastical?

Then beside his feet on the carpet his eye picked out something: a stain. It was suddenly like a message from Kitty; he remembered vividly her speaking of the stain in the drawing room of the train, of the blood and how it haunted her. He reached down to touch it, but it was perfectly dry.

The *femme de chambre* must have missed it. Feeling a bit foolish, he got down on all fours and sniffed it: gin. Someone had spilled a martini on the Turkish carpet. It was not likely that Kitty had spilled it. He did not know her to drink frequently or to excess. It must have been a guest. Suddenly he knew there had been more to the closeness of the room than lack of air. He had smelled cigarettes, strong Turkish ones. Kitty did not smoke. At least, he had never seen her do so.

He got to his feet, feeling panic. They knew no one in Istanbul. Someone, a stranger to him at least, had been here in the room with Kitty. And for the smoke to have lingered in the sitting room meant it had not been that long ago.

He began feverishly searching the suite. When he entered the bedroom, he saw it. If he had only bothered to go into the bedroom before instead of perfunctorily looking in to see if Kitty were there . . . A large white envelope with his real name, Stefan Blauer, lay on the great double bed, untouched by the maid.

He rushed over to it and tore it open. It was in perfect German:

Herr Blauer,
    Miss Hammersmith is with us.
    We suggest a fair exchange: your lovely "wife"
for the Grail.
    We shall contact you.

The signature of the star of David shook him; he
had begun to think of the Jews as his natural allies
now. He was confused. So much so that only slowly
did it dawn on him what they were demanding: the
Grail, the Phoenix Formula, for Kitty's safe return.
And, of course, he did not have it. What had made
them think he did? How did they even know about it?

Then almost immediately, as if in answer to his
questions, the telephone rang. He grabbed for the bedside phone and picked it up.

"Blauer?"

"Yes," he replied, almost stammering.

"Miss Hammersmith is safe." It was a woman's voice
speaking German with a slight accent. "You will
please bring the Grail with you to the Café Le Bosphore in Galata— do you know it?"

"Yes, but—"

"Miss Hammersmith will be waiting for you in your
rooms when you return."

"Wait! Wait! I don't have it, I tell you. *They* have
it."

"That is most unfortunate, Herr Blauer. How very
sad. How tragic for Miss Hammersmith."

Blauer thought with lightning speed. It was useless
arguing with them. They were desperate—and why
shouldn't they be? His beloved Fatherland had made
them so.

"Wait! I'll do as you say. Café Le Bosphore."

"Quite correct. *Auf Wiedersehen.*" The woman hung up.

Her intimate, romantically tinged farewell hung ironically in the dead air of the telephone line. Blauer put the phone back on the receiver. It made a hollow, clicking sound.

They had not even bothered to give him any assurance that Kitty would in fact be released. It was obvious that they knew he was in love with her, enough in love with her to give up his own life.

But they didn't even want that.

The Café Le Bosphore was a stylish, international café in the heart of the foreign banking quarter. But unlike a Parisian café, it had an extensive garden in the back, shaded with fig trees and great potted palms. In one corner of the courtyard garden played a small string orchestra, more Viennese than Turkish, except for the presence of a Turkish zither which once an hour, as if as a reminder, would play a Turkish popular song, although in the softest, most Western tones.

The café interior was all etched mirrors and modern-style columns tipped with the Egyptian influence of a lotus. Blauer could see himself reflected prismatically throughout the café as he walked through to the garden. He glanced at his watch. It was a little after five P.M. English, French, Greek and Turkish families were taking tea, but the full crush of clients would not come until after seven o'clock, when businesses closed and *l'heure de l'apéritif* began. He took a last glance at himself in the mirrors, noting the duly conspicuous black leather satchel he was carrying as a ruse for his contact, and stepped into the garden. He found an empty table and sat down.

Whoever it was would find him; he had no worry about that. He put the satchel under his chair as if for safekeeping. It would look unnaturally evident on the small café table. He ordered a Turkish coffee and sat back to wait.

The small string orchestra simultaneously struck up an all too familiar melody: *"Der Wind hat mir ein Lied erzählt."* He had heard it sung the evening he had met Kitty in Berlin. He caught no negative reactions among the many couples and single customers clustered about the courtyard. A few couples, Levantine and not Germanic-looking, got up to dance the slow tango being played as if the dance itself were not a bit passé and the song pungently, romantically Thousand Year Reich.

Blauer felt strangely calm. He was not sure what he would do when the Zionist contact arrived. He had his small revolver in his pocket, but he was not sure what he could do with it in such a crowded place. He had become totally fatalistic, he realized, since his return from the Caucasus.

His calm soon vanished as Kitty flashed before his mind's eye. Her beauty, her quiet and not-so-quiet defiance when her will was ignored, her integrity, and now her innocence played with his emotions in a savage manner. He had been a selfish fool to entangle her in this Grail business. And yet it had all seemed a game at first.

Blauer tried to get a grip on himself.

The tango ended to quiet applause and the zither began to play. Scanning the garden, he caught sight of someone coming out into the courtyard in a rumpled white linen suit and Panama hat. The stout figure looked familiar: Reginald Cranston-Jones. He made a comical figure of a man as he crossed the garden, looking this way and that. He seemed to spot no one he knew, and then he caught sight of Blauer. His rotund face broke into a broad smile as he strode toward Steven's table.

Blauer's amusement vanished, to be replaced by

panic. He did not want Reggie sitting down with him. His Zionist contact would never put in an appearance with someone else at his table.

"How are you, old man! So good to see you again." He pulled up a chair and sat down uninvited. A waiter rushed over. "A tea, please. And a few sandwiches and things," he said, idly rubbing the fingertips of one hand together in midair. "What have you been up to in Istanbul, Mr. Blauer? And where is your charming wife?"

"Kitty? She's doing some shopping."

"A woman's fondest pleasure. Funny I haven't run into you two before now."

"Well, we only got here recently. We . . . we decided at the last minute to get off the train at Budapest and spend some time there."

"How Germanic of you, my dear Blauer. Though I should say Austrian. Loving gypsy music and all that." Reggie's tea things arrived.

Blauer nodded hesitantly. He had no idea whether it was a favorite Austrian tourist area or not, but he did not really care. Even if Reggie were trying to trip him up, what did it matter? Blauer looked around the garden, trying lamely to hide the desperation he felt. A tall, thin Jewish-looking man entered, and hesitated at the entry to the garden. Blauer stared at him, his heart pounding. But the man spotted a table of friends and, with a smile, went over to join them.

"Then you missed that dreadful business near the Hungarian-Rumanian frontier."

"What?" Blauer turned back to face Reggie's inquiring face. He thought he caught an odd smile around the eyes.

"Yes. A man fell off the train, it seems. Very messy indeed. The train made an emergency stop. And then later a body was found in one of the first-class parlor suites. Shot to death." Steven stiffened, then relaxed. He did not like the way Reggie was looking at him.

There was something mocking in it. Perhaps the fat Englishman knew that it was his suite. But why should he toy with him then?

Steven began to smile slightly as it dawned on him: Reggie was the Zionist contact. He had to be. Or if not the actual contact, he was checking out the rendezvous point, making sure there were no detectives, no ruse.

"Sounds awful. Glad we missed that. Sounds to me like a gangster movie."

"Or a spy thriller," put in Reggie. "By the way, Blauer, where did you pick up that handsome satchel you've got under your chair?" Reggie reached down and felt its leather.

Steven was stunned at Reggie's boldness, and then relieved by it. There was no doubt in his mind now. Blauer reached down under his seat and pulled the satchel out of Reggie's touch, then brought it up and sat it in his lap.

"Nice leather, isn't it?"

Reggie was finding it difficult to control his eagerness to grab the satchel, to open it, to actually have in his hands the mysterious object that would give him power, himself and his people.

The sound of the zither ceased. The string orchestra struck up a fox-trot. Couples flocked to the dance floor.

"Too bad Mrs. Blauer isn't present. I'd ask her for a dance, if you wouldn't mind."

Steven felt a spasm of rage take hold of him; he gritted his teeth and took a deep breath.

"Something wrong?" Reggie's face was all solicitude. Steven brought himself under control. His hand felt inside his jacket pocket. The revolver was cool and inviting. Reggie was pure sadist; he could put a bullet through him with not a twinge of conscience. For a second he wondered what twisted a man like that; and then he knew the answer. Blauer felt a certain shame.

"No, nothing. Just a chill." He attempted to change

the subject: "I'm surprised to see couples dancing at this hour."

"Don't they have *thé-dansant* in America? Tea dances? So civilized, really. I'm quite surprised."

"If we do, I've never been to one." As Blauer spoke, he fingered the satchel. Reggie riveted his attention to it. "Oh, I forgot. You asked about the bag. Got it in the neighborhood. Can't remember the name of the shop."

"Oh, what a pity. Can I hold it for a minute?

Blauer froze. The game was over.

"No, I don't think so, Reggie," he said slowly. Reggie's face paled. He sat back, feigning surprise, or perhaps it was genuine. "I'm afraid you've tipped your hand."

"What do you mean?"

"This." Blauer had taken the palm-sized revolver out of his pocket and slid his gun hand behind the satchel in his lap. Only he and Reggie could see it.

Reggie moved his hand toward his pocket.

"Think again!"

"Just getting my handkerchief." Beads of perspiration had broken out on Reggie's forehead.

"Forget it!"

"Come now, dear boy," Reggie began, sitting back slowly in his chair. "You wouldn't do anything rash in here."

"Try me."

"Let us just make our little trade and—"

"There's no trade to be made. I'd just as soon kill you on the spot. I've got nothing to lose, old chap."

A look of consternation broke out on Reggie's face. "Don't be an ass, Blauer. The Grail isn't worth it. You know it's better off in our hands than in theirs, and if you keep it, they're bound to find you and kill you in a flash."

"Oh, they may kill me, all right. But I don't think they'll get the Grail from me."

Reggie heaved a sigh of exasperation. "You *are* naive."

"I don't think so, my friend. They already have it."

Reggie reacted as if struck by lightning. He made a grab for the satchel.

"Hold it!" Reggie froze in midair. "I don't think it would be wise for the whole café to see this gun I have pointed at you, now would it? Then I might as well take the pleasure of killing you and have it done with."

"How do I know you're not lying?"

"What difference does it make?"

"You'll never see Miss Hammersmith alive."

Blauer flushed with anger. His gun hand moved.

"If you want to see her again . . ." Reggie's voice was cool, deliberately sinister.

With his free hand Steven reached in his pocket and pulled out a large Turkish bank note, which he left on the table.

"You're going to take me to her. Stand up." Steven switched the gun to his pocket but made it evident that it was aimed carefully at Reggie. Then he stood up, holding the satchel in his left hand. Reggie got to his feet with amazing speed. "Please, you first, Reggie," said Blauer with a smile.

They left the café. A line of taxis was waiting outside, and Blauer motioned Reggie to get into the first one. The driver jumped out and came over and shut the door behind them with the usual solicitous bows, then moved around quickly and got in the driver's seat.

"Your destination, *efendim*?"

"It's your call, Reggie."

"Platta Gate." His voice was sharp, clipped. The driver touched his forehead and started the motor. In minutes they were skirting the Golden Horn and heading for the New Bridge.

"Care to take a look inside the satchel, Reggie?" Steven handed it over to him. Reggie fumbled wildly at the clasp, then opened it.

The look of shock registered on Reggie's face was pure pleasure for Blauer. Steven burst into laughter.

It was empty except for two brass hotel ashtrays for weight.

Although it was only six in the evening, the staircase leading to the room near the Platta Gate was negotiable only by touch. The stench was overpowering.

"You couldn't have picked a better location?" Blauer asked at the heels of the heavily panting Reggie.

"It was none of my idea. It was hers."

Before Blauer could question as to who the woman in question was, Reggie let out a curse.

"You bloody bitches. Not enough sense to keep the door bloody shut!" Reggie pushed the door open wide and stepped into the attic room. He stopped dead in his tracks.

"What's wrong up there?" Instinctively Blauer felt for his gun. Reggie did not answer. Steven pulled the gun out and readied himself to shoot. He rushed up behind Reggie and pushed the heavy man to one side.

A scream rushed to his throat, but never emerged. Furniture lay smashed all about. Blood was splattered on the floor and walls, seemingly still damp.

"Oh God. No. No. God! Oh my God!" Blauer's stunned repetition whispered, moaning, in the low-ceilinged room. Reggie, when Blauer had shoved, had lost his balance and fallen to the floor like a rag doll. He sat staring up at Blauer.

Strewn across the cot were the bullet-riddled bodies of Olga Bartok and Kitty Hammersmith.

"She was one of us," sounded Reggie's voice hollowly. "So was your father, my boy, in the end . . . It was a good fight."

"But quite ended!" Kriegshofer stuck the barrel of his machine gun into the small of Blauer's back. He began to laugh uproariously. Strang and Häger moved into the room behind the Reichsführer.

Chapter Eleven

The Rolls-Royce Silver Shadow had been exchanged in Istanbul for a curtained Mercedes-Benz berlin similar to the limousine which had taken the three high-ranking Germans to Templehof Field. With Herr Strang at the wheel, there was plenty of room in the back for Blauer and Silver to fit between Kriegshofer and Häger.

The curtains on the rear and side windows were drawn against any prying eyes. A motorcar thus enclosed provoked little interest in the streets of the city. It was assumed that wealthy Turkish women were being whisked from one part of Istanbul to the other in *purdah*. Though the veil had been outlawed, Atatürk had not insisted that the Turk put his women on public display either.

The bound and gagged Blauer and Cranston-Jones could be taken anywhere in the city without arousing attention; they were invisible; as invisible as a man's hareem.

"Herr Sebottendorf was a man of wisdom in some ways. But he forgot, I'm afraid," continued Kriegshofer to Häger, "that the sins of the father as well as his talents may be visited on the son."

"History will allow a place for the Blauer traitors, father and son."

Kriegshofer smiled, laughing softly as if to himself. "The perfect bourgeois firm: Blauer, father and son, traitors. And perhaps history will also give a footnote to young Turkish gigolos who prefer being paid by a man for information than by a woman for pleasure." From the driver's seat, Strang had joined in the humor laughing in the controlled manner he produced for his own dry wit.

They had crossed the New Bridge over the Haliç and were motoring through the streets of Galata, congested with shipping business and businessmen leaving their offices for home. Strang drove with particular caution. This was no time for the slightest accident, the least commotion. And they were in no hurry.

The curtained berlin finally came out on the avenue which ran along the Bosporus up toward the Black Sea at a point relatively free of trade and traffic.

Trees shaded the avenue. Warehouses and shipping offices had given way to homes, which became larger with more luxurious grounds the further up the Bosporus the car went.

Reggie and Blauer had long since ceased to show any signs of struggle. They had not been given much opportunity for it from the outset. It was all too obvious in the blood-splattered garret that if Kriegshofer chose he could have them machine gunned on the spot. Strang had bound and gagged them with a relish that was almost sensual. The ropes were pulled just tight enough to reach the threshold of pain; the gag pulled back into the mouth, across the tongue, just taut enough so that if there were any attempt to speak, to shout, a spasm would occur in the throat. Reggie had vomited once and was reminded clinically by Strang that if he chose to struggle he would simply choke to death, his windpipe clogged.

Kriegshofer had, in the full flush of his victory, decided to toy with his prey. Blauer had no illusions as to a humane outcome to the Reichsführer's sport. They were not meant to live much past their destination.

Yet what remained to him of his life seemed sweeter, more precious than he could have imagined. Knowing that death would come shortly, he had no need to agonize suicidally over the death of Kitty.

Kriegshofer's gloating, his braggadocio, his taunts of treason washed over Blauer, making no impression, leaving no trace at all. He barely heard.

Steven remembered the old belief that before death a man's life passed before his eyes. In this case it was the contemplation of his life by a condemned man awaiting execution. It was slow; it could, if he allowed it to be, be painstaking. But for once in a life which had not allowed for much self-satisfaction or true joy, Blauer granted himself peace of mind. His affair with Kitty took on symbolic proportions: he had loved her, he had known love completely in these last months of his life.

Perhaps it was the intolerably brutal, cosmically unjust events that he had witnessed in the past month which prompted it, but he found himself believing for the first time in the opposite of this absolute evil on the march in the world. He believed now in the good, if not in God, in a plane of existence after death, if not in heaven. He would rejoin Kitty—he was as sure of it as he was of his own imminent death.

"You should be glad to know, my dear Blauer—" Kriegshofer paused to catch Steven's undivided attention. He gave Blauer a short, stinging slap like a whiplash across his face to insure it. "You should be glad to know, as a former citizen of the Reich, that the Führer's campaign in Poland has been successful beyond our wildest hopes. The entire country is ours. The Wehrmacht has done its job splendidly," he nod-

ded to Blauer in mock homage, "and is about to be
replaced by our own men, who will dispose of the
country as befits the racial and spiritual goals of the
Reich."

Enough confusion was evident in Blauer's eyes for
Häger to begin to laugh.

"*Mein Reichsführer,* our Herr Blauer seems ignorant of the goals of the Reich. Should we not enlighten
him?"

"It would seem that we should, Häger. If only as a
courtesy. Actually," Kriegshofer paused, his face aping
well the furrows and creases of a professor deep in ana-
lytic thought, "the universal goals of the Reich are
known to only a select few, an elite. Some thought you
were by nature born to that elite, Blauer. I myself was
never that foolish. And I was proved correct."

Blauer's eyes flashed a denunciation of Kriegshofer's
words. For a split second Steven realized that he still
had clung to the belief in the primal goodness of his
country: he had, like some wandering knight of old
robbed of his lands through treachery, thought of himself as representing the true, the good Germany, the
true elite. Where had this idea come from, he wondered briefly: from his father?

The sense of Kriegshofer's words would soon strip
him of those illusions.

"There is to be no Poland. As a bestial, inferior
race, polluted with Jewish and Asiatic blood, its labor-
ing elements shall be allowed to breed in order to provide disposable labor for the Reich. But those elements which, alas, have been crossed with Aryan blood
must be liquidated: that genius in their blood which
has made them rise exceptionally over their race must
be exterminated as thoroughly as one would any error
in a genetic experiment.

"Even now solid Tyrolean stock is being readied to
migrate into the northern slopes of the Beskid Mountains. The frontiers of Asia are to be pushed back."

Kriegshofer paused to contemplate Reggie for a moment. His eyes had grown glazed, his face glistened with perspiration, his body was numbed by the terror he nurtured in the factually based imaginings of his brain.

"Jews—that is another problem. For the moment we round them up in urban centers. They do not put up much struggle, degenerate as they are. Some are to be shipped further east. Eventually, of course, they must be exterminated once and for all. But the Führer does not wish to antagonize world opinion with stories of atrocity. Neither the British nor the French seem to care to move readily to war in defense of their Polish allies. This is splendid. And perhaps war can be avoided," Kriegshofer's voice diminished to a mystical whisper, "until we are ready for the swift coup de grace which the recovery of our ancient covenant has made possible."

The three Nazi officers sat in silence for the next few minutes. What they had witnessed of the Grail's power in the Caucasus had awed them. The belief in their Aryan glory had been further transported to cosmic heights.

Strang pushed down lightly on the accelerator. The berlin picked up speed. There was virtually no traffic on the road, only an occassional car, a bus or a horse cart.

Before Blauer in his mind's eye stretched the blackened crater of an entire valley wiped off the face of the earth as if one of the Nordic giants had used it as a fire pit to roast his dinner of a whole ox impaled in his great spear.

As the fantastical image grew in his mind, Steven compared Kriegshofer to this Nordic giant. A stifled laugh escaped through the gag, making a repulsive gurgle like that of a man without a tongue. Without realizing it he had slipped to the brink of hysteria.

Häger's eyes flared. With the flat of his palm, he

struck Blauer's face three times rapidly in succession.

"The *Schweinhund* should be liquidated, *mein Reichsführer*. This waiting . . . the Jew pig and he would be corpses now in the garret. We could be flying back to Berlin."

"Silence, Häger." Kriegshofer's command echoed in the fast-moving car like a gunshot.

Reggie began to whimper. Häger took out the rebuke by his commander on him, striking Reggie's face from side to side until he bore the red imprint of his hand on both cheeks.

"Pick up speed, Strang. Herr Häger has a point. We are wasting precious time."

"*Jawohl, mein Reichsführer.*" A smile played on Strang's face. Like Kriegshofer, he relished the imminent pleasure of watching their two prisoners tortured to death as a sacrifice to the Grail at the hands of the former Ottoman headsman placed at their disposal by the honorable Ibrahim Pasha. His anticipation verged on the pornographic; an erection pulled his trousers tight across the groin.

But the berlin was not far from its destination. The great mansion of Ibrahim Pasha, a reconverted Ottoman fortress high on the cliffs overlooking the Bosporus on the eastern side and a few miles to the north of the mouth of the Black Sea, was now visible up ahead. The grounds of the mansion were surrounded by a high stone wall. The great gates were of wrought-iron work. The car pulled to a halt before them. Strang sounded the horn. Immediately a powerfully built Turk in his early twenties, in baggy pantaloons and broad sash but with a Mauser machine gun strapped over his shoulder, came out of the gatehouse and opened the grounds to the car. As the berlin passed, he gave them the fascist salute.

"Is the Turk an Aryan, *mein Reichsführer?*" quipped Strang.

"And is Signor Mussolini?" Kriegshofer laughed

outright as he answered. The three Nazis laughed together now in the comradely manner of the old storm-trooper days in the beer halls of Munich. Nostalgia came quickly to all three of them, stunned and elated as they were by the heady glories of the present and the immense triumphs, presaged now in Poland, which awaited them in the future as masters of the world.

The berlin moved slowly up the tree-lined gravel path to the door of the mansion, then came to a halt. A tall black-haired man with a closely clipped mustache, dressed in an expensively cut three-piece suit, stepped out of the house to greet them.

"*Heil Hitler*," he said, a warm smile of hospitality on his face, as Kriegshofer stepped out of the car.

Kriegshofer returned the smile and saluted.

"*Heil Hitler*, Ibrahim Pasha."

He admired the wealthy Turkish aristoctat's stature, his lean, angular jawline, the fine prominence of his cheekbones. Ibrahim Pasha could well have been an Aryan, except that he was a Turk, one whose blood-line was carefully recorded going back to before the fall of Constantinople. Strang had posited an interesting dilemma as they had entered the grounds of the mansion. What were they to do with these loyal but non-Aryan comrades? And the Japanese? But that would have to be a struggle for generations far in the future. Today *lebensraum* only meant pushing Asia back from the river Oder to the Urals: that would be enough for his, the first generation of the master race.

"You have them, Herr Kriegshofer?" Ibrahim Pasha had descended the four steps from the main door to the gravel and now gripped Kriegshofer with both his hands on the Reichsführer's shoulders.

Kriegshofer raised his arms and clasped his Turkish host with great pats of both hands. Still clasping Ibrahim Pasha's arm in one hand, he gestured with the other toward the car: "I have them indeed."

Strang had gotten in the back seat as a rear guard,

prodding Blauer and Silver out of the car after Häger.
Their limbs were cramped from the tightness of the
ropes binding them, and they were unsteady on their
feet.

"Everything is prepared, my good friend." Ibrahim
Pasha turned his attention away from the two prisoners and back to the Reichsführer. "I have summoned
my eldest son to witness the executions. I take the
words of your Führer to heart: 'We shall encourage
the growth of a violent, domineering, intrepid, cruel
youth.'"

Kriegshofer nodded soundly; then a smile crossed
his face.

"But the Turk, my good friend, has always enjoyed
a healthy reputation in this regard."

"We are warriors, Herr Kriegshofer. Just as you
Germans are warriors. And who knows, perhaps one
day your genetic investigators will find that our races
stem from the same root."

Kriegshofer shrugged his shoulders and smiled. "It is
very possible, Pasha. I should like to know that we are
brothers."

The two men entered the house, followed by their
prisoners, who were prodded along between Strang
and Häger. In the immense two-story reception hall,
Ibrahim Pasha stopped. He pointed toward a small,
heavy wooden door. "I suggest your men take the prisoners down to the cellars. Mehmed has prepared everything and is waiting now . . . with great impatience,
I might add." Ibrahim Pasha's amusement was visible
only in his eyes.

"*Jawohl, mein Reichsführer*," saluted Strang without waiting for the order.

Reggie began to whimper. Häger laughed and
shoved him toward the door. Blauer accompanied
Strang in silence as the SS officer threw open the door,
and Häger shoved Reggie before them.

* * *

If the idea of seizing the Grail for himself had ever passed through the mind of Ibrahim Pasha, he had never entertained it. He did not have the knowledge to decipher the runes inscribed on it. He did not have a massive following in a powerful country to make its potential a reality. Though he was not alone in his desire to see a strong, fascist Turkey, he and his friends made up a minuscule minority, most of whom were in reality only nostalgics of the Sublime Port and the Ottoman Empire.

The role which he had actually played—as protector of the Grail in Turkey—would prove much more fruitful. Already the gratitude and esteem of one of the most powerful men in the Reich was his.

And in a stroke of genius he had thought of the ideal piece of music to accompany the executions. That morning he had sent several of his servants into Istanbul to search for the recording he required. He had had an electric cord run down into the dungeon chamber, where the spectacle would take place, lit by torches stuck in iron sconces in the wall (he knew well the Nazi predilection for the medieval). And then he had had the Victrola brought down and placed discreetly behind a great swastika banner, which he had had hung from the ceiling and two feet out from one wall.

In the center of the room had been placed the machinery of execution: the racks, the hooks and trusses and a small wooden table on which were laid out various instruments, including bastonades and his own private collection of Ottoman whips.

On an altar erected before the banner, immediately on being removed from his personal safe, would be placed the Grail in its plain ebony case. Opposite that wall chairs were arranged for five spectators.

In a few minutes the execution spectacle would begin. Ibrahim Pasha clapped his hands abruptly. The Turkish headsman, a squat, powerfully muscular man,

bare-chested, wearing the traditional sashed pantaloons, his head ritually shaven clean, entered the
room, leading his two victims behind him. Strang
leaned forward in his chair to catch the expressions on
the faces of Blauer and Silver, alias Cranston-Jones.
The three Germans were surprised to see that the prisoners had not been prepared in any special way, except that their gags and ropes had been removed: they
were still both in street clothes.

Simultaneous with the entry of the headsman came
a servant bearing a tray with four goblets and a bottle
of champagne. Kriegshofer had been shocked by the
age of Ibrahim Pasha's son, a boy of only eight, but
was pleased to see that the child would at least not be
given champagne to drink. The boy sat bolt upright in
his armchair, like the adults. His face was impassive
until the headsman entered. Then a look of terror, it
seemed to Kriegshofer, passed over the boy's face, only
to be quickly controlled and hidden.

"I should like to propose a toast of victory," began
Ibrahim Pasha, rising to his feet. "To the victories of
the Reich in Poland, to the final victory of the Reich
and the Grail." All stood, including the boy, and the
men toasted and emptied their goblets.

"*Sieg heil*," said Kriegshofer, his glass drained.
Strang and Häger echoed him: "*Sieg heil!*" The servant collected the goblets on the tray and left the
room. The Germans regained their seats, as did the
boy. Ibrahim Pasha looked about the room with
haughty pride, then clapped his hands.

The executioner moved forward and took hold of
Blauer. Steven struggled instinctively against the
Turk's viselike grip, then took control of himself and
submitted.

Reggie's face jerked in a reflex spasm. His eyes were
wide and his skin glistened with sweat as he watched
the executioner strip the jacket off a now passive
Blauer and then bind his outstretched arms to the up-

right rack, but not his feet. For a second Reggie experienced hope, relief. They were not actually interested in him: what had he ever done directly against them? But once Blauer was bound to the rack, the executioner turned to Reggie. A chortling sound came out of the powerful man's throat. Silver opened his mouth to scream, but the headsman had moved forward immediately and clamped the Englishman in a bear hug which took the breath out of him. The scream died in his throat.

The needle of a phonograph stylus came down on the groove of a record. The dungeon room echoed suddenly with the crackle of static and then the first Wagnerian chords of the Good Friday Music from *Parsifal* filled the room.

All three Germans made no attempt to hide their surprise and then their pleasure. Kriegshofer leaned over to Ibrahim Pasha and whispered his thanks and congratulations in his host's ear, then sank back in his armchair and closed his eyes briefly to savor the majestic music of a piece conceived in homage to that very Grail which was now before them.

He opened them again abruptly as a scream of terror erupted from Reggie's throat. The executioner had turned Reggie upside down like a side of meat and hung him by both feet from two hooks which had stabbed through both ankles and were then hung up from chains suspended from the ceiling.

Häger, as did Kriegshofer, Ibrahim Pasha and the boy, still sat back in their armchairs, but Strang had leaned forward so as not to miss the slightest spasm as Reggie's body twitched in midair, but in silence. Silver had blacked out.

The headsman picked up a knife from the table. Blauer screeched a sound of rage and strained at his ropes until his hands were nearly blue from the cut-off of circulation.

"Kriegshofer, you'll burn in hell!" Blauer finally

managed to scream hoarsely. The spectators, including the boy who did not understand what Blauer said, laughed.

With the razor-sharp knife the Turk cut Reggie out of the husk of his clothes. The Englishman hung there oblivious, a pasty white mass of soft flesh sprouting reddish hairs here and there, while his shoes and spats remained on his feet. The headsman wafted a small bottle of spirits of ammonia around Reggie's nose and mouth, and the Englishman revived, only to let out a long wail of pain.

Kriegshofer noted the victim's reaction with interest. The once excruciating pain of the hooks pierced through the ankles had obviously numbed that part of the body sufficiently for the torture to continue, although blood did continue to drip in rivulets down the legs and over the thorax, shoulders and arms onto the stone floor.

Strang was slightly disappointed, although his genitals were suitably aroused. He felt the headsman had gone to extremes too swiftly: the execution would never last as long as he had hoped. Then he caught sight of Blauer and understood. It was Blauer who was really being tortured, first mentally and later physically. Strang sat forward with much more eagerness. The spectacle was magnificent, a first-rate tribute to the Grail and its power.

Ibrahim Pasha gestured to the servant peering out from behind the swastika banner to increase the volume. The headsman had chosen one of his favorite whips, a flagellum of the old Roman style, its rawhide strips studded with small iron thorns. The Englishman would bellow like John Bull himself when the first lash struck. The increase in volume was essential. He did not want the music totally interrupted.

Blauer watched in agony as Reggie screamed over and over from the blows of the lash. He strained at the ropes binding his wrists to the rack. And then he felt all rational control vanish and his body possessed by another force which began screaming in unison with Reggie and thrusting his body forward in great yanking spasms, as if his whole body were periodically flung out in the air on a swing.

Reggie's flesh was soon a flayed, bloody mass, but the Englishman had not passed out again. The pain was perfectly set on the threshold, noted Kriegshofer with open admiration now for Turkish methods.

Unable to restrain himself, Kriegshofer put his hand down on Ibrahim Pasha's arm, which lay outstretched on the arm of the chair, the wood carved at the end in great lion's claws gripped in his fists with excitement.

"We Germans have something to learn from you after all, my good friend. We are perhaps too mechanized, a bit too modern."

Ibrahim Pasha turned to Kriegshofer and smiled briefly, then turned his attention back to the spectacle. He had witnessed nothing quite like this since his own father had taken him to an execution of traitors during the Great War. At the age of twelve he had almost vomited at the sight of the blood, then had grown impassioned, drunk with it, then awed by the spectacle of death. It had taught him much about life. He hoped now that his young son would learn as much.

Deliberately he had not looked at the boy, granting his son the privacy of discovery. Now, however, something out of the corner of his eye pulled at his attention. He glanced over at his son beside him. The boy sat rigid in the armchair. His small knuckles were white from gripping the arms of the chair. His small, gentle face was ashen. But it was the boy's eyes which suddenly alarmed him: they were glazed over as if dead. He reached over and shook his son by the shoulder. The small body was stiff, cold. Slowly Ibrahim Pasha got up, almost as if in his sleep. He did not wish the majesty of the moment disturbed. He knelt down

in front of the child. He shook him violently. His
shoulders, chest and arms moved, but his hands were
frozen in their grip on the chair. And then suddenly
the grip was freed. The child's body tumbled forward
out of the chair, onto his kneeling father.

From out of Ibrahim Pasha's throat came a wail
which echoed in the death chamber and overpowered
the blaring chords of *Parsifal* and the screams of
Blauer and Silver.

Kriegshofer stood up immediately and rushed over
to his host and stood over him helplessly, uncompre-
hendingly. Strang and Häger followed their Reichsführer. Then the servant behind the swastika banner ran across the room, shouting something in
Turkish which stopped the executioner as he readied
his whip for another blow. The guard at the door of
the chamber, the same young Turk who had let them
in the gate, still armed with his Mauser, now rushed
forward to join the crowd around the kneeling father
and the small stiff body of the boy.

At first Blauer had no idea what was happening.
Then instantly he gave a desperate yank at the ropes.
One of them snapped. His right hand was free, though
his wrists were raw and bloody almost to the bone. He
felt no pain, only exhilaration. He pulled and rubbed
the rope around his left wrist against the metal of the
rack. The rope held fast. Pain lashed through him as
he gave it all his strength, almost blacking out. It
snapped free.

Blauer stood there, immobilized. All backs were to
him. Reggie hung like a carcass in a butcher's shop; he
had finally fainted again—or perhaps he was dead.
And then Blauer noticed the wooden table with its array of torture instruments. They were only a few feet
away. His head swam. He sucked in his breath: the
pain was clouding his mind.

He lunged to the table and seized the knife and an
instrument which resembled a medieval mace. In a

split second he was behind the guard with the machine gun. He shoved the knife into his back and left it sticking out as if it were in a slab of butter. With his left hand he brought the mace crashing down on the young Turk's skull. The cranial bone crunched and shattered. Blood spurted out of the split skull. Blauer wrenched the Mauser off the falling man's shoulder and stepped back several feet as the others turned around with questioning expressions at the sounds of the young Turk's death rattle.

And then they all froze.

Steven felt a wave of hysteria lap at him. He wanted to laugh at the look of shock on their faces. And then at the fear, the fear of sure death, its face the black hole of the machine gun's muzzle.

Coldly he opened fire. Their screams now echoed in the room as the needle caught in the last groove of the record and sputtered its slip, slip, slip into a suddenly silent room.

Blauer stood staring at the carnage before him.

He had no recollection of himself as himself, Stefan Blauer, until he found himself running down the gravel drive to the great iron gates. Under his arm was the ebony box from the altar before the swastika banner.

He had the Grail.

Easily he found the latch on the gate and pulled one wing of it open and slipped out. He was on the great, tree-shaded avenue. From far in the distance he thought he heard a shout. He threw the Mauser back inside the gate. It clattered onto the gravel drive.

For no particular reason he chose to run to his left, then stopped running and continued walking. There were no pedestrians as yet, but cars passed by occasionally. The sun lay low in the sky, an enormous orange ball on the horizon, ready to set.

He came out on a side street off to his left, little more than an alleyway, which ran steeply down to the shore of the Bosporus. He ducked down in. He did not stop to think; for the last twenty or so minutes of his life, he had been acting solely on instinct.

At the foot of the road, off to his right, he spotted a landing and a ferry, one of the ubiquitous ferries which zigzagged their way back and forth and up and down the Bosporus. He found change in his pocket, paid his fare and stepped on the boat. The steam whistle tooted a few minutes later.

As the ferry pulled out, he stood at the railing watching the shore. A man ran toward the dock. Blauer turned abruptly from the railing and went inside. He had not identified the man, but he hoped that the man, whoever he was, had not spotted him.

Reggie had been right after all when he had said that he would have a hard time safeguarding the Grail. Now he hoped mercifully that Reggie was dead.

Blauer held the ebony box tightly under his right armpit as he held both hands thrust deep into his pockets to hide his torn, bloodied wrists.

He could not return to the Hotel Ozipek. He was alone in Istanbul. His wrists began to ache with pain. He wondered if he could turn to Kemal.

No, he would have to go it alone. He could no longer involve others. Kitty was dead. He would not have Kemal dead as well.

When the ferry docked diagonally down the Bosporus, he got out on the Asian shore. He could not run the risk that the man rushing toward the departing ferry had been someone from the house of Ibrahim Pasha.

He would have to get back to Istanbul, then off, free, somewhere with the Grail, on his own.

On his own. The words now echoed in his mind. They were absurd.

Chapter Twelve

He had the Grail.

As time separated him further and further from atrocity and living nightmare, reason began once again to resume its normal functions. Under his arm he had the key to all the bloodletting, slaughter and holocaust he had witnessed in the past month.

As the ferry had made its last docking in Istanbul, he had disembarked feeling giddy, exultant. He had miraculously saved his own life; he had saved the Grail. He was free. He was alive. He had triumphed and come back from the dead as surely as if he had actually crossed over to the other side. The dungeon room became fantastical in his mind.

Around him people moved easily to their destinations. As he passed through the streets, men talked idly at café tables, fingering worry beads, savoring the cool evening breeze. Trees rustled over the avenues. Street vendors hawked their wares in elaborate chants. Everyday life, even in this foreign city that was half in Europe, half in Asia, was sweet, soothing, good.

Blauer had become ecstatic.

The garret, the dungeon room—they were unreal. They belonged to another universe. His reason rejected the full impact of their reality at first, then began to make him doubt their reality at all. The horrors were seeping slowly away into a fog of amnesia: the mind in its own way was healing, soothing.

But he had the Grail.

He had reached deeper into the right-hand pocket of his trousers (he had not taken his hands out of his trouser pockets since boarding the ferry) in search of money. He felt bank notes. He pulled them out and began counting them openly as he walked unsteadily (he had no idea he was unsteady) down the tree-lined avenue. Passersby eyed him oddly, some pityingly, some with alarm: the young European has smoked hashish, obviously, and was out of his senses to be walking about flashing a great amount of bills.

Blauer had difficulty counting them, then gave up and thrust them back in his pocket. He did not once notice his wrists now, or feel them.

A few of the pedestrians had averted their eyes. One of them pointed out the young European in the crowd to a policeman, but by the time he had spotted Blauer and blown his whistle, his figure had vanished around a corner. No complaint had been registered; the policeman returned to directing traffic in his previous haphazard but authoritarian way.

Blauer had moved through Istanbul like a ghost.

He wandered the streets in aimless celebration of freedom and living. He sat for a moment on a bench in a park. He listened to his heart beat as if it were music. The moist night air took on molecular qualities before his eyes, like so many microscopic bubbles, which only he could see, dancing before his eyes. The rustling of leaves, the percussion rhythms of the crickets and locusts, the cries of night birds filled him with an inexplicable joy.

It was nearly midnight before his fatigue struck him suddenly in an onslaught which nearly made him drop in the street. He had no idea where he was. The night-

mare of his situation licked at his heels. He stumbled
further on down the narrow streets of shuttered shops.
The occasional street lamp seemed to layer him in
gray dust. He pulled out the bank notes and, for the
first time since he had deliberately buried them in his
pockets on boarding the ferry, he saw his wrists. They
horrified him. They did not seem part of him. They
were numb, disengaged from his body. But as he stared
at the torn, scab-encrusted flesh, he felt the first sig-
nals of pain reach his brain. And at the same time his
left arm, which had held the Grail to his body with
viselike strength began to ache.

He must find a place to sleep before he collapsed in
the street. He moved on, his wrists carefully, deliberately hidden in his pockets. He was as ashamed and
fearful of them as an escaped prisoner would be of
manacles or leg irons.

And then he saw a sign printed in Latin letters:
HOTEL. He did not try to make out the rest. It hung
over a great windowless door, set in a windowless wall.
The dreamlike nature of the moment became over-
whelming. Blauer drew his hands out of his pockets.
He tried pulling his shirt cuffs over his wrists: it
worked; they were hidden. He pulled at the door. It
was locked. He began rapping, then pounding on it
painfully.

Finally from behind the wall he made out a voice
which seemed to be yelling back to him and coming
closer. A crossbar seemed to be drawn back with a
thud; the heavy door creaked open inward. A dark,
thin, sleepy-looking man in what looked like pajamas
stood staring at him, blinking against the glare of the
street lamp. In his hand he held a wooden club.

"Hotel?" Blauer pronounced the word slowly, hesitantly.

The man nodded and motioned him inside, grum-
bling to himself and to Blauer, who could not understand a word, with relief that outside the door had not

been a thief, a murderer, a djinn, but only a European tourist. He could charge more for the room, pocketing the difference for himself.

The cobblestoned courtyard was humid and foul-smelling under the perfume of the pines. Opposite, light streamed out of an open door.

"English?" The lean, bony night porter turned to face Blauer from behind the hotel desk, pronouncing the word in two syllables so far removed from each other that Blauer did not understand at first.

"Yes, English."

"Sign, please," the night porter parroted, pointing to a line in the register. Careful not to disclose his wrists, Blauer pulled out his right hand and signed. Every stroke of the pen sent a stab of pain up his arm.

"Five pound," announced the night porter, his expression now harsh, almost menacing.

Vaguely Blauer realized that the sum was enormous, even for a room in a first-class hotel. He reached into his pocket and felt for a bank note, then pulled it out carefully so as not to disturb his shirt cuff. The night porter's eyes lit up with pleasure at the sight of the note, five pounds, then betrayed disappointment. He had hoped to argue a bit, to bargain. The night porter became suspicious.

"Luggage?" he mispronounced. He repeated the word again.

Blauer finally understood: he gestured toward the ebony box under his arm. The night porter grunted and scuffed out from behind the desk. His sense of hospitality had returned; he would give this tourist the best room.

The room was only on the second floor, but the stairs exhausted Blauer so that he became dizzy and thought he might black out or fall. The night porter, shining an oil lamp ahead of him, did not notice and plodded up the worn wooden stairs. With a large iron key he opened a door which was a smaller version of

the door on the street and held the lamp high to illu-
minate the room. Blauer saw a large wooden bed; he
groaned softly to himself. The night porter entered
and set his oil lamp down beside the oil lamp on the
bedside table. He pulled out matches, struck one and
lit the lamp.

He turned toward Blauer and gave him a broad,
harsh smile: "Good night, mister." He pronounced the
words carefully, almost sensually, but made no move
to leave the room. He stood grinning at Blauer.

At first Steven was confused, then remembered that,
although he had not carried up any bags, the man was
expecting a tip. He reached carefully into his pocket
and drew out some coins and offered them in his palm
to the night porter. The man showed surprise, then
nodded what appeared to be thanks and took the
coins. Then he stood before Blauer as before, grinning.
He said something in Turkish in a soft voice.

Blauer shook his head to show he did not understand.

Slowly, deliberately, his eyes never leaving Steven,
the night porter reached down and grabbed hold of his
crotch in his left hand. He seemed to squeeze slowly
for a moment, then released his hand.

Blauer lost control. He began to laugh hysterically.
The night porter, alarmed at the noise, made hushing
sounds. Blauer gasped for breath, then continued,
though more softly, making the spasms of sound between sobbing and laughter.

The night porter shrugged his shoulders but showed
no malice, only a renewed indifference, and left the
room.

He had left the iron key in the lock on the inside.
Blauer rushed to the door and turned the key. He
stood still for a moment in the middle of the room,
then took the ebony box out from under his arm.
Holding it in both hands, he realized with surprise
that it was quite heavy. He laid it down on one side of

the bed and then his own body on the other. A voice
in his head told him to remove his shoes and the rest
of his clothes, but then he fell immediately into a
deep, heavy sleep.

Strang made to move his toes, then his fingers.
Nothing seemed to be broken. He gave a shove to
Kriegshofer's blood-drenched body. It rolled free of
him, but the pain of the exertion shot through him so
fiercely that he nearly blacked out. He looked down
at his side: it was drenched in blood. Gingerly he fingered over the place and found the wound. A bullet
from the Mauser had passed through his side. But that
seemed to be the only wound he had sustained.

He heard a groan. He looked around him among
the tangled, bloodied bodies. None seemed to move.
Carefully he extricated himself and staggered to his
feet. The moan sounded again. He looked around and
then found the source.

Reggie still hung by his heels from the hooks. His
head twitched slowly from side to side. He was semi-
conscious. A grin spread over Strang's face. He reached
down and pulled the knife out of the Turkish guard's
back.

Reggie's moaning drew him like a siren's song. At
the side of the fat, naked body suspended in mid-air,
Strang contemplated the slowly turning head, the face
nearly purple from the unnatural drainage of blood to
the head. He stroked almost gently down Reggie's side.
The eyes flickered open. They focused on Strang with
little comprehension. Then they widened in recogni-
tion.

Strang laughed. He held the blade of the knife before Reggie's eyes. Suddenly fear raged through Reggie's bloated face. His eyes bulged further out of his
head.

Strang put the razor-sharp blade to Reggie's throat.

A gurgle erupted from the punctured esophagus. Reggie's body writhed in a spasm, then hung limp.

Strang's blood raced in his veins. His face was flushed. He felt with his left hand down onto his crotch. Then he glanced up from his victim to the swastika banner on the far wall.

The Grail was gone.

Terror seized his whole body and mind. He had not thought of that before. It was gone. His future was gone with it, unless he recovered it.

Blauer had taken it. Rage swept through him. He glanced down at his boots. They dripped with the blood spurting out of Reggie's throat and mouth and nose.

With his full fury he kicked Reggie's lifeless head violently.

Blauer woke up as dawn broke over the city. The rattling wheels of carts grinding on the cobbled streets, the voices of vendors hawking, the loud moan of the muezzin calling to prayer, reached him as he rolled over onto his back and then felt the edge of the ebony coffer in his side.

He jerked bolt upright.

He had slept in his clothes, even in his shoes. As the memory of the last twenty-four hours flooded through his brain, he was seized with panic, then relaxed. Unwittingly he had stumbled into a place where no one would think to find him. He began to laugh softly to himself like a madman.

He reached down, despite the pain in his wrists, and unlaced his shoes, then kicked them off onto the floor. He got to his feet beside the bed and stripped off the remainder of his clothes, then, naked, crawled into the bed under a sheet.

He rolled over on his side and placed one hand on top of the ebony coffer. He had to sleep.

* * *

The majordomo of Ibrahim Pasha's household was the first of the servants to come upon the massacre in the cellar.

Strang began issuing orders immediately. Suleyman would immediately contact all of Ibrahim Pasha's political friends; the murders would be avenged, and avenged immediately. He did not tell Suleyman about the Grail and of its having been stolen. The murderer was a renegade German, a traitor, he explained. The police were not to be called in until after the meeting. It was essential that everyone be there within an hour.

Suleyman bowed and went to Ibrahim Pasha's study. The names of the Muslim Brothers were in a notebook in the wall safe. He worked the combination, pulled out the notebook and began using the telephone. The operator came on finally. Suleyman arranged for the operator to stay on the line until all persons had been contacted. He would come the next day when he was free and receive a handsome gift. The operator made the Istanbul telephone lines work to amazing perfection.

In a little more than an hour, all the Brothers who were available were assembled.

Strang's English was not equal to oratory, but it was sufficient for the purposes of the meeting. Those who could not understand English had his words explained to them by friends who did understand.

Strang introduced himself vaguely as a high-ranking German official, a friend of Ibrahim Pasha and of Turkey. In silence he led them from the entry hall where they had gathered, down the staircase to the dungeon.

The reactions of the mullahs and the other Muslim Brothers were as expected. They were particularly enraged by what appeared to be the murder of the boy.

Standing on the dais of the altar, the great symbol

of the Reich behind him, Strang began to speak after yelling for silence.

"The traitor, the murderer, is still in Istanbul. He must be found. But he must not be killed until what he has stolen from this house is recovered. It is a black box of ebony. It contains material of major importance for the victory of Germany and of your own Turkish cause. The box must not be opened.

"Under no circumstances are you to open the box. You are to return it to me immediately.

"The traitor's name is Stefan Blauer. He must be killed, but only after the black box is recovered. He must not be allowed to speak to the police."

Strang circulated a photograph of Blauer in Wehrmacht uniform which had been in SS files. He himself had only known Blauer from this portrait, before seeing him in the flesh in the garret room near the Platta Gate. It was an accurate portrait.

"The search must begin immediately. Do you have any questions?" There were none. The Brothers, after conferring among themselves, translating, explaining, understood their duty immediately: vengeance. The additional search for a black box was a quirk of the German, but they were loyal. They would do as Strang had asked.

Strang gave the Nazi salute. To himself he said: *Heil Hitler.*

He beckoned Suleyman to him as the Brothers filed out of the dungeon.

"Yes, *efendim*," the graying, slightly bent servant bowed.

"You shall call the police once this equipment," Strang gestured toward the racks, the table, the hooks and Reggie's body, "has been removed. Get rid of the body of the fat one before the police arrive. You are not to mention me or the Brotherhood. Tell them only that it was a political murder and give them this photograph of Blauer."

* * *

Blauer woke up again. He had no idea what time it was, except that as he went to the window and looked through the cracks in the shutters, the courtyard below seemed to be lit by the full light of day.

He still felt weak. It had to be exposure to radiation in the Caucasus.

He dressed, picked up the ebony coffer and unlocked the door. The hall was dark, illuminated only by a small window at the far end, but it was quiet. No one seemed to be on the floor.

Steven shut the door behind him and went down the hall to the staircase. If possible he wanted to leave the hotel unnoticed.

From the last landing before the ground floor, he peered down. There was no one behind the desk. The hotel seemed deserted. Quickly but quietly he descended the remaining stairs and crossed the reception room and stepped out into the courtyard.

The light was blinding. Blauer figured it was past noon. And the great wooden door was open. With deliberate speed he crossed the courtyard and stepped out into the street.

As silent and bleak as it had been the night before, the street was now the opposite. Horse carts creaked by one after another, loaded with furniture, alfalfa, sacks of rice, anything imaginable. The occasional car on this narrow street honked and stopped-and-started its way through the traffic, the pushcarts, the street hawkers, through the customers going in and out of shops; men leaned idly against walls, talking, sleeping.

Blauer had no idea where he was going, but it was easy to lose himself in the crowd. He followed the street until it merged into a tree-lined avenue. He remembered the avenue vaguely from the night before. He assumed that he was in Galata. Sitting down at a table outside the first café he came to, he ordered a coffee. He put the box down gently on the seat of the other chair at the table.

The coffee arrived, hot, black and thickly Turkish. He drank it down, then also emptied the tumbler of water served with it. An elderly but well-dressed Turk at a nearby table was reading a paper.

Steven wished he had a paper, an English-language newspaper, not a Turkish one. And then the man folded a page over and began to read a following page. Blauer caught his breath. Staring back at him was a picture of himself in Wehrmacht uniform taken only a few months before; it seemed like years before, a lifetime before. Steven panicked.

So one or all of the SS men were still alive. It seemed unbelievable.

Weird thoughts assailed him as he left a few coins on the table, picked up the box and moved rapidly off into the moving stream of pedestrians before the man reading the newspaper had a chance to recognize him. The SS men had to have supernatural powers: bullets did not kill them. Like vampires, a stake would have to be driven through their hearts to destroy them. They were not men but deadly phantoms, wraiths. They were creatures of the devil.

Then reason took hold of him again.

He had to get hold of a newspaper. He had to read the story behind the photograph.

He walked with his head lowered slightly, his face turned away from people sitting at tables in front of cafés. Then, out of the corner of his eye, he spotted headlines on a newspaper in English. He suddenly felt delirious with hope: it was an omen from heaven. He had been given what he had asked for in his heart.

The newspaper seemed to have been abandoned on the tabletop. He went over casually, picked it up and walked on along the shaded sidewalk.

The horns of motorcars and buses honked almost continually. Radios in kiosks would blare out wailing,

harsh, rhythmic popular music or the voice of a Turkish announcer. Steven prayed that his picture was in
the newspaper folded under the arm with the ebony
box. He looked for a bench, a park, in which he could
read through it.

Fate did not seem as benevolent toward this wish as
it had been toward the one for the newspaper. Growing hunger and necessity to read the paper finally
forced him to sit at a table inside a small restaurant.
He picked the darkest corner table and sat down.

Perfunctorily he ordered shish kebab, and then
buried himself in the newspaper. Almost immediately
he found the article describing the massacre for political reasons of a well-respected Turkish gentleman.
Blauer's picture, the photograph of the murderer,
stared back at him.

He only half ate his meal and left the restaurant. He
hailed the first taxicab he saw and got in.

"Mister?" questioned the driver with a broad smile.
Steven had no idea where he wanted to go. He was
simply convinced that he was safer from identification
in the taxi. For a moment Blauer panicked.

"The bazaar," Steven muttered.

"Efendim?"

"The Great Covered Bazaars, please."

The driver touched his forehead and moved off into
the traffic.

He *was* in Galata after all. He recognized some of
the buildings, the streets, and soon the taxi was crossing the New Bridge and heading toward the Old City.
Gradually Blauer noticed something odd about the
streets, and the traffic. The congestion was lessening.
Fewer and fewer cars were in evidence. The streets became relatively quiet. Fewer people crossed or walked
the sidewalks. He glanced at his watch: it was a little
after three o'clock.

Panic seized him and this time remained with him.
It was time for the traditional afternoon siesta; the

streets were clearing of people. In an hour Istanbul would be nearly a ghost town.

He would be as obvious on the street as a snowman in July. And, if they were hunting him, which they surely must be, both SS agents and police, he would just as quickly be destroyed.

The taxi was now pulling up alongside the northern part of the bazaar. There were still people on the street in this quarter. With some relief he paid the driver after haggling for nearly five minutes. This time, however, he appreciated the time used up.

Once night fell he would be safer.

Everything had changed since he had learned that the police were seeking him. That factor precluded checking into a hotel. Knowing that he was a foreigner, they would have every hotel in Istanbul covered.

He got out of the taxicab and headed into the bazaar. The narrow, roofed-over alleyways echoed with blaring radio music, a female voice quivering, then wailing over the metallic notes of the zither. Voices bargaining rose and fell. But the shops were closing. Little by little the alley was emptying of people. Shutters were being bolted. Men were gathering in the shops to drink tea and eat from trays of food brought by shop boys or to smoke.

Blauer pushed on further into the bazaar. He passed the tin merchants, sellers of pots and pans, then crossed through one street of the rug merchants and entered the streets of the goldsmiths. Progressively as he walked there was less tapping of hammers on gold. He increased his speed.

He had no destination, simply to lose himself in a bazaar which soon would be nearly empty. He walked faster still, then began to run.

A man came out of his shop and stared at him. He began to yell after him in Turkish, then yelled to his fellow shopkeepers. Blauer broke into a dead run.

Perhaps because he was running the man thought he was a thief. Or perhaps he recognized Blauer from the newspaper. Steven turned the corner into another alleyway and began walking at a normal pace. He was among the rug merchants again. Behind him he thought he heard voices yelling to each other, racing after him. He ducked into a shop.

"*Efendim,* you are welcome, *efendim.* But soon we close. Please look. Look." The shore, balding merchant, his arms spread wide in hospitality, smiled broadly, but his eyes scoured him intently.

Blauer flinched slightly under the man's stare, then smiled back and began slowly to look through the piles of rugs. "You wish to put down your box? Such a nice box, *efendim.*" The man had his hands on the ebony coffer.

Abruptly Blauer pulled it out of his grip. "No, thank you. It isn't heavy . . ." The man eyed him oddly. "I'm afraid that if I put it down I will forget it," Blauer said and smiled. The merchant smiled back and shook his head. He did not understand. Blauer had spoken too quickly; the sentence was too long. Rather than repeating, Steven continued smiling and began looking at the rugs again. The merchant followed behind him as Steven painstakingly examined one rug after another, pile after pile. The man had stopped talking. He was growing impatient.

Finally the merchant shrugged his shoulders and gestured toward the back of the shop.

"I take my tea, *efendim.* Please call." The merchant bowed. Steven smiled and nodded.

"Thank you. I won't be long."

The man scuffed in his slippers into the back of his shop and sat down. He clapped his hands and a young boy appeared. He said something to him, and the boy ran out.

Blauer succeeded in calming himself; he would have to assume that the shopkeeper was not sending the boy after the police. He continued looking over the rugs, slowing down his examination as much as he could, playing the connoisseur, all under the nearly disinterested gaze of the balding merchant.

There was a rustle. Steven reeled around.

It was the boy. He entered the shop, breaking through the beaded curtain in the back entrance, carrying a tray with two glasses of steaming black tea. Blauer grinned in relief. The merchant raised an eyebrow.

"You take tea with me, *efendim*, please. It is my honor."

Blauer shook his head and continued smiling as he turned back to the rugs.

"*Efendim*! Please, you take tea with me." The man's voice was insistent. Blauer looked up at him. He realized he had no choice; otherwise he risked insulting the rug merchant. And he needed him desperately as an ally.

"Yes, thank you, sir," began Steven, walking toward the back of the shop.

"Blauer!" The voice bellowed his name.

Steven turned around slowly. He had heard the voice before; perhaps it was Kemal.

Facing him at the entrance of the shop was Strang. The lean face of the SS officer grinned at Blauer's look of shock. Strang pulled a revolver from his pocket.

"You are dead, Herr Blauer."

The blast of a gunshot filled the shop. The merchant screamed. Blauer lay on a pile of rugs, dazed for a second. But the bullet had not touched him.

Steven rolled over and then instantly up onto his feet, leaving the ebony coffer on the rug. He hurled himself across the room, aiming at Strang's legs.

The SS butcher toppled onto the floor. They wrestled, Blauer on top of him. Strang still held the gun in his hand. It went off, lodging a bullet in the ceiling.

In the split second of shock at the noise of the shot, Blauer brought his fist crashing into Strang's face. He wrenched the gun out of his hand and tried to get to his feet. Strang grabbed hold of Blauer's belt. Instantly Steven pointed the gun at Strang's head and fired.

The SS man's hands shook in a spasm as they still clung to Blauer's belt. A black hole lay open in Strang's forehead. Blauer turned his eyes away and wrenched himself free and onto his feet.

From outside the shop he heard the thud of feet rushing toward the shop. Suddenly the entry filled with Turks. One of them yelled a phrase over and over. Steven caught the word "Pasha." As he moved to turn and head out the back through the beaded curtain, the mob which had gathered rushed him. Blauer turned back and fired wildly into the crowd.

There were howls of pain, screams. The mob fell back. Blauer turned and raced out through the beaded curtain into the back alley, snatching up the ebony box on his way.

"Halt!"

He heard gunfire. Screams and yelling suddenly filled the bazaar on all sides. Men and boys poured out of the shops, then after yelling to each other, began converging on the shop of the rug merchant.

Blauer hid his gun in his jacket and, holding the box to him, huddled against the wall. He inched his way forward, turning his face away as a small crowd ran past him.

By a stroke of luck they had not identified him with the gunshots. He bolted off in a dead run.

He continued running. He had no destination. He had even lost track of the way out of the bazaar. Then up ahead he spotted what appeared to be a mosque. He rushed to the entrance, then stopped. Inside he could hear the noon prayers being recited.

Quietly he slipped inside the door. A guardian

pointed to his shoes. Blauer did not want to remove them, but he had no choice. He bowed his thanks to the guardian and bent down to unlace them.

Row upon row of Turks bowed to Mecca.

With eyes averted in an attitude of reverence, Blauer slipped to the rear of the mosque, his shoes clutched in his arms along with the Grail. The low murmur of the prayers calmed him. The Grail. He still had it. For a second the thought crossed his mind that once it was in his hands, it would stick with him like glue.

He had to get out of Istanbul.

His mind suddenly cleared as if for the first time since the sight of Kitty's body in that ramshackle room.

The Bosporus was constantly crisscrossed by ferryboats. He only had to get to one of them and cross over to the Asiatic side, much the same way as he had escaped the day before. But with one difference.

Strang was dead.

Blauer walked slowly and quietly to a side entrance, put on his shoes and stepped out. He was on a street outside the maze of the bazaar. He hailed a taxi and got in.

Brandishing a large Turkish bank note, he made the driver understand that he wanted to take a ferry across the Bosporus. Steven was shocked to find that the taxi took him there in five minutes.

He could have walked it. He paid the driver, then stepped up to the ticket window for the ferry. He avoided looking at the clerk face forward so that he would not be recognized from his picture in the paper. The clerk noticed nothing, yawned and pushed forward his ticket and change over the counter.

In minutes he was on the ferry.

Blauer stood at the rail, flushed with his success as the boat pushed off from shore. Suddenly he froze as he felt a hand come down lightly on his shoulder. He reeled around, his hand rushing toward the gun in his pocket.

"Don't you recognize me, Mr. Blauer?"

The face of Ramyan Langsung beamed back at him. "We meet again in good fortune, Mr. Blauer. Your father may rest in peace."

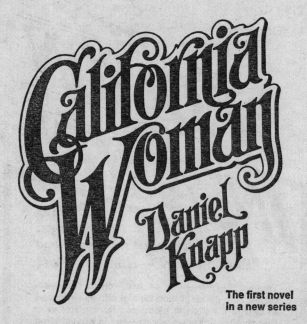

CALIFORNIA WOMAN

Daniel Knapp

The first novel
in a new series

A sweeping saga of the American West

Esther left New England a radiant bride, her future as
bright as the majestic frontiers. But before she could reach
California, she had lost everything but her indomitable
courage and will to survive. Against the rich tapestry of
California history, she lived for love—and vengeance!

A Dell Book $2.50 (11035-1)

Comes the Blind Fury

John Saul

Bestselling author of *Cry for the Strangers* and *Suffer the Children*

More than a century ago, a gentle, blind child walked the paths of Paradise Point. Then other children came, teasing and taunting her until she lost her footing on the cliff and plunged into the drowning sea.

Now, 12-year-old Michelle and her family have come to live in that same house—to escape the city pressures, to have a better life.

But the sins of the past do not die. They reach out to embrace the living. Dreams will become nightmares.

Serenity will become terror. There will be no escape.

A Dell Book $2.75   (11428-4)